His Tarnished Ruby

The Scottish Stone Series, Book Three

Kelsey McKnight

His Tarnished Ruby

Limitless Publishing, LLC
Kailua, HI 96734
www.limitlesspublishing.com

Formatting: Limitless Publishing

ISBN-13: 978-1-64034-214-9
ISBN-10: 1-64034-214-1

Dedication

This is for all the lovely readers who have followed me through London, into the Highlands, and back in time. I'm pleased to have you on another adventure. And to my fellow author, Sarah Fisher, who always helps me keep the bosoms heaving.

If for the heart's own sake we break the heart, we may

When the last ruby drop dissolves in diamond light

Meet in a deeper vesture in another day.

Until that dawn, dear heart, good-night, good-night.

–A Farewell by George William Russell

Chapter One

Flora MacLeod smiled over the rim of her goblet at Jasper MacNee, who answered with a brazen grin, flashing his straight teeth and deep dimples. She sat up straighter and pretended to be interested in someone at the far end of the MacLeod's feasting hall. As much as she'd like to march over to his table and have him take her into his arms, her friend Penelope Elmsly—now MacGregor—had told her time and time again that a man would never fancy a loose woman, but one worth a bit of a fight, and this was exactly what Flora intended to give Jasper.

She trained her eyes on the newlyweds, Penelope and Drummond, who looked ridiculously in love. Flora could remember how awkwardly the pair had interacted when they first met. Drum was a silent giant, frozen when in Penelope's queenly presence. Penelope had been positively bitter toward him in return, almost rudely uninterested in his constant company.

But out of hundreds men in London, not a single one was prime husband material for Flora. Of course she had always held a flame for handsome Jasper, but Conner never allowed her to pursue him. He thought Jasper was too old and too poor to sustain the life Flora led. She had tried to forget him by seeking out every eligible bachelor Penelope knew, but none could compare to the fiery man back in Scotland with the loud laugh and broad shoulders. The British men were too reserved and soft of hand. How could she respect a husband who had paler skin than her, and a softer voice?

She flipped her hair over her shoulder and glanced back at Jasper, trying her hardest to look as appealing as the scullery maid beside him. While Jasper tipped his cup at her and shot her another jovial glance, she thought she had turned his head. But his gaze quickly slid back to the busty beauty who offered him more meat. He could hardly spare Flora a second look, which burned her pride.

That cad. That braggart. That handsome devil.

She sighed and dropped her goblet back to the table, feeling embarrassed at being so obviously slighted. Her pressed blue silks had been altered for a more daring neckline and she even donned a string of pearls to draw the eye down toward her modest bust, hoping to temp Jasper to sample *her* goods, and not the common maid's. Nonetheless, he hadn't noticed the way she batted her lashes in his direction, nor the way she sent each servant to his table with the finest foods. It had been Flora who'd sent the maid with her dish to him in the first place, not thinking that Jasper's wandering eyes would be glued to the woman in the plain brown dress.

However, she counted her blessings that no one

2

saw how easily a serving wench, who forwent her stays to sway freely beneath her gown, turned her beloved's head. With her rather humble bust, Flora felt as if she paled in comparison to the curvy woman who currently held Jasper's rapt attention.

Although she tried to look away, she found her stare drawn to them and she bit her lip as the maid tilted her head back to laugh at something Jasper said, showing off her long neck. Flora felt her fingers itch as she longed to put her hands around that maid's throat. But, as Penelope often reminded her, a man wasn't attracted to a slovenly wench with rough edges, but by a smooth gem who shone in their presence.

"Yes," Flora muttered, "but some men seem to like a rocky shore upon which to dock their ships."

"Where have you gone?" Gwen asked, waving her hand before her older sister's face.

Flora jumped and turned to her. "Nowhere."

Gwen already knew. She reached under the tablecloth and grabbed her hand. "Jasper's a fool."

She felt her face heat. "Pardon me?"

"I said he's a fool and a flirt. You think no one notices the way you stare, but *I* do."

Flora felt a sharp sting in her chest. "He's just talking with her to be polite. It means nothing. It's what men do…they flirt."

Her little sister hummed and released her grip. "If you say so."

"What are my wee sisters whisperin' about?" Conner questioned from behind them.

"Nothing of consequence," Flora replied, draining her goblet of wine and waving a servant over for more.

"Aye?" Conner asked, not sounding entirely convinced.

"Aye," Flora said sternly.

"Is there a secret?" Little Ian, the MacLeod's ward, popped his head between the two sisters, his mouth full of stolen wedding cake. "Please tell me!"

"There's nothing to tell," Flora hissed through gritted teeth, holding her cup aloft for a fresh topper of drink. "Go on and get some more cake."

"Leave them alone!" Charlotte called from the other end of the long table.

Conner looked over his shoulder at his wife and nodded before turning back to Flora. "Do us all a favor and try no' to stare at that buffoon all evenin', aye?"

Flora felt her cheeks burn up, but she lifted her chin and tried to look unaffected. "I don't know what you're speaking of."

Charlotte shot up from her seat and snaked through the guests to reach them. She slapped her husband firmly on the arm with her closed fan. "Shoo, Conner. You're the only buffoon I see."

"Ach, wife, I'm the man o' the house and the laird o' the castle," Conner stated rather dramatically. "Ye should—"

"I said shoo, now *shoo*!" Charlotte held up her fan again and Conner slipped away, laughing. She turned back to Flora. "He always loves to rile me up, no matter the situation."

"He always did to us, before you," Gwen told her, smiling fondly.

Charlotte leaned into Flora, placing a thin hand

upon her shoulder. "I've been watching you this whole evening and I think it's time you take a stroll about the hall, yes?"

Flora huffed through her nose. "I'm quite well here, thank you."

"You're going to be quite drunk in a moment," Charlotte replied, snatching Flora's goblet and handing it to a passing servant. "If you're too far with drink to properly dance later, you'll regret it."

She knew Charlotte was right. If there was anything her sister-in-law was an expert in, it was the joys and pains of alcohol. Flora stood, a bit shakily, and hooked her hand through the crook of Charlotte's arm.

"Let's go greet some of the guests, yes?" Charlotte said. But her inquiry was only a formality, as she was already leading them toward Penelope's mother, Cecily Elmsly.

"Darling *hic* Charlotte! Dearest *hic* Flora!" Cecily squealed, sloshing her wine over the rim on her glass and into a dish of butter. "What a *hic* glorious occasion. I never thought I'd see the *hic* day."

Flora grinned, holding in a bout of giggles. If Charlotte thought *she* was a bit tipsy, then Cecily was positively ready to fall down drunk. She knew Cecily would be fit to burst with excitement over her daughter's wedding, but she thought that the old woman would at least be able to consciously participate in the merrymaking that followed.

"Oh, posh." Charlotte waved a hand in the air. "We all knew Penelope would find a good match in the end."

"And what a *hic* fine match she made!" declared Cecily, gripping Flora suddenly by the wrist. She was surprisingly strong for such a drunken old thing. "Now it's your turn! Time to catch *hic* the *hic* bouquet!"

"Not yet, Cecily." Charlotte gently plucked the woman's bony fingers from Flora's arm. "I'm sure Flora will tell us when the time has come for her to marry."

"Yes *hic* yes," Cecily muttered before Ian scampered under the table, followed by a pack of castle mutts. "Goodness, me!" She gripped the edge of her chair as a particularly large dog bumped against the bottom, making her topple to and fro. "What on earth was that?"

Flora laughed openly, a bit too giddy with drink to keep it in any longer. "That was merely wee Ian and his dogs."

"And he just cured your hiccups, it seems," Charlotte pointed out. "Well, we must be off. Lots of introductions to make."

As soon as they had left Cecily, Flora leaned in toward Charlotte. "My, I've never seen her so gone. All of society poise went away with the wine."

"She's been waiting for this moment since Penelope's birth," she explained, her gaze flitting from one face to another. "Finding her a suitable husband has been her life's work. Now she's quite retired."

Charlotte steered her deeper into the crowd, which parted in their wake. No one wanted to accidentally bump the Macleod's wife, nor his younger sister. Although personally, she could do with a certain *someone* bumping against her as often as he pleased. Flora knew Jasper wasn't too afraid to graze against her in the hall or whisper to her in the hidden corners of the castle walls. But those were secret murmuring of adoration, not public declarations. If only he would only make his intentions clearer and…

"Oh, poppet!" Charles Brandley, Duke of Fenton, flew from his seat and took Flora's free hand, crushing it in his. "So darling to see you."

"Charlie, you made it," Flora cried. She was so pleased that one of her dearest friends from London had come to celebrate Penelope's wedding. She had missed his constant cheer.

"He came in quite early this morning," Charlotte told her. "I had him placed in one of the second floor guest rooms."

"Would I miss a bash in a castle for dear Penelope?" Charlie chuckled. "Hardly! Besides, I couldn't pass up the sight of some good ol' Scottish thigh."

Charlotte's head tipped back in laughter but Flora followed Charlie's gaze to the bared knees of one of the men, who sat wide-legged on a bench. Charlie was always a fan of the Scottish ways of dress, especially if he saw some muscles between the swatches of plaid.

"I was just taking Penelope on a turn about the hall, care to join?" Charlotte asked.

"Oh, no. I'm quite…*occupied* at present." He raised his orange brows and slid his eyes downward to where one of Penelope's cousins, Matthew, sat twiddling his waxed mustache.

7

"*Matthew?*" Charlotte hissed, her hazel eyes wide.

"Yes, we met on the train. Charming fellow. We have *much* in common," Charlie replied with a cheeky grin.

"Well, you get back to that." Flora giggled, pulling Charlotte away.

"You know what they say about weddings—full of romance," Charlotte muttered.

"I'm not certain that I would call it romance."

"Look, there's Andrew Philips." Charlotte nodded toward a group of young men crowded in a corner.

Flora wracked her brain, feeling as if she might know the name, but not terribly certain. "Who?"

"You've met him before, at Penelope's..." she paused, then lowered her voice, "her engagement party to Theodore Harrison."

Flora shrugged. The name still meant nothing. "I suppose I should remember Andrew Philips, but I don't."

"Then let's make our reintroductions." Charlotte stopped before the group, who all turned and bowed their heads slightly.

"Good evening, Lady MacLeod," one short and stout man said.

"Good evening, Lord Grey. Gentlemen, this is my husband's sister, Flora MacLeod." She gestured to Flora, who bobbed her head and smiled sweetly, making note of each man.

"Flora, do you remember Andrew Philips?" Charlotte held her hand out to a tall and lean man with dark red hair and wide brown eyes.

"H-how do you do?" Andrew said quietly, taking Flora's fingers and pressing them to his lips with shaking hands.

Flora had a sudden shot of remembrance. She had met a stuttering man at the Elmsly home in London. Penelope had sworn to her that Andrew didn't have a speech impediment, yet there he was, stumbling over his words. Although, he wasn't terrible to look at; his skin was clear, his lips full, and his eyes seemed to hold flecks of gold around the irises. Flora thought he might be capable of some merriment, if he weren't so much like a jittering bunny in the hunt.

"Lovely to see you again." Flora allowed him to press her hand once more before slipping it from his grasp. "How do you find Scotland?"

"M-most agreeable," Andrew told her, his gaze darting about the room. "I find the entire c-country fascinating."

Flora glanced to her right, seeing that Charlotte had quite abandoned her. But as she looked for her sister, she caught sight of Jasper, who was staring at her under furrowed brow. If she knew any better, she would think the fiery Scot was jealous. Well, if he was happy enough to cling to some tart in a low-necked gown, then Flora was well within her rights to walk with a suitably dressed gentleman like the proper lady she was.

"Mister Philips, might you take me on a turn about the room?" she inquired with the breathy, well-practiced voice all men in London seemed to love. "It seems Charlotte has disappeared."

Andrew swallowed audibly and cleared his

throat. "C-certainly." He held out his arm for Flora to take and she was surprised to find she felt sinewy muscle beneath the fabric of his jacket and not the boney limb she expected.

They strolled along the edge of the hall, arm in arm, in complete and utter silence. Flora was always one to talk, but she couldn't stomach the thought of prying conversation from the man. It would feel positively cruel to subject him to such things. But as she cast furtive glances in Jasper's way, her heart beat a little faster in her chest. Jasper looked positively livid. His cheeks were almost as red as his hair and his head was turned completely away from the busty maid.

"Serves him right," Flora whispered to herself.

"W-what was that?" Andrew asked.

She hummed daintily, slightly embarrassed at being heard. "Lovely night," she replied amiably.

"Yes."

Flora paused again, growing tired of the awkward stroll. "Are you staying on in Scotland long?"

"Only a, um, until t-tomorrow."

"How terribly lucky."

"Lucky?"

"Why, yes. I long to return to London, but with both Penelope and Charlotte here, I hardly have a reason to return."

"W-well, with winter approaching, the c-country's a finer p-place to be."

She stifled a yawn. She despised chatting about the weather and wished she had finished that last glass of wine. "All the same, I much prefer the bustle of London. Do you keep a full-time residence there?"

"Yes, a small one while I'm, um, s-studying."

"Your parents don't reside in the city?"

"No-no, they l-live in Brighton."

"The seaside town?" Flora had recalled Charlotte telling her how she and Conner had stopped there during their honeymoon.

"Yes, they have a hotel."

"That's rather grand." She glanced up at him, his face looking forward, steady and still. If he sounded like a flighty bird, he certainly didn't look it. His jaw was strong and angular and Flora spied a small shaving nick along the sharp bone. It slightly marred his pure complexion. He was not pale in the womanly sense, but Flora suspected he spent more time at his studies than other men his age might have. She felt it a pity that such a face spent time stuttering indoors, as she thought him more than handsome enough for the soft likes of the British girls.

Still, she wouldn't say he was her type, for all his pleasing features. None could hold a candle to burly Jasper. Although, the pair did have one slight similarity. Andrew's hair was a deep red, a sharp contrast in hue from Jasper's flaming orange, but still in the same family. It was almost as if the colors mirrored their personalities; Jasper was bold and flashy while Andrew more reserved and steady. The shade of his brushed-back locks made her wonder if he had some Scot in his blood.

"Mr. Philips," she began, "where do your people hail from? British through and through?"

"Y-yes. Kent, mostly, besides my parents, as far back as can be accounted for."

"Oh, and you said you were currently focused on your studies. What is your area of interest?"

"Law, madam."

"Oh, so you mean to be a barrister? That's—"

"Good evenin', lad," Jasper's deep voice called from behind. "Might I steal the lady away for a dance?"

Flora felt heat prickle the back of her neck as she turned toward him. "Hello, Jasper. This is Andrew Philips. Mr. Philips, this is Jasper MacNee."

"Pleasure," Andrew said to Jasper in a voice much deeper and sturdier than the one he used with Flora. Strange how men could do that, change their voices so. She thought the more masculine pitch suited him better and almost wished it was there to stay.

"Now we've gotten that out o' the way, I'd like to take the lady for a dance, aye?" Jasper took Flora's free hand, pulling her to his side before Andrew could answer.

"Lovely speaking with you, Mr. Philips. If I don't see you again before you leave, have a pleasant journey back to London." Flora allowed him to kiss her hand before watching Andrew bob a short bow and retreat into the crowd.

"I saved ye, did I?" Jasper grinned widely, looking down at Flora.

"*Saved* me?" She laughed, clutching to his arm. "Hardly. We were just having a pleasant chat. Don't tell me you were jealous?"

"Jealous o' that dandy?" he asked, gesturing with

his thumb. "Do no' make me laugh! That's akin to me sayin' I'm jealous o' a wee barn cat."

"Don't poke fun."

"Have a soft spot for him, then?" His eyes narrowed, crinkling at the corners.

"Don't be daft. Now, I believe you asked me for a dance."

"Well, aye, I did." He nodded and leaned back on his heels. "But I also promised the lads another round."

Her breath caught in her throat. Was she being brushed aside for a bunch of men? "Pardon me?"

Seeming to catch his mistake, he smiled at her, showing the set of dimples he knew she loved. "Besides, if the MacLeod came to find me and his wee sister dancin', there's no tellin' what he'd do."

"I-I suppose you're right," Flora admitted somewhat sourly, releasing her hold on his arm. It was true that her brother was not too keen on the thought of Jasper courting her. Nonetheless, she still felt slighted at her promised dance being taken away, no matter the reason for doing so.

"There's a good lass. Now, we'll be sure to get in a dance o' our own soon enough, when no one's around to see us, aye?"

"Yes, yes," she whispered quietly as he turned away from her and strode back to his table.

For the second time that night, Flora felt ignored by Jasper. She was sure he had feelings for her—surely he did. Since she reached the marrying age nearly two years ago, he had pursued her, albeit quietly, murmuring words of love into her ear and promising a quiet country life full of children and animals. She wondered whether he might have already proposed, without Conner's constant interferences.

Flora pondered this as she weaved through the crowd back to her own seat. But as she neared Jasper, she saw he had more company than just "the lads." The maid was once again perched upon his knee and twirling a lock of his bright orange hair around her finger in a rather coy manner. Flora turned up her nose, flying past them in a hurry to reach the safety of the MacLeod family table.

"He's done it again?" Gwen asked her as Flora fell into her seat.

"See for yourself," she replied shortly. She looked for her cup before remembering that that Charlotte had taken it.

She glanced into Gwen's goblet and saw it was still filled to the rim. Quickly, she snatched it, holding it to her lips and beginning to drink. Gwen said nothing, merely raising her brow as she resumed her conversation with the woman on her left.

The wine was fragrant with late summer honey and coated her tongue with its sweetness. As she watched Jasper whisper in the maid's ear, she felt her jealousy rage anew within her and the drink did little to calm it. Before she knew it, her goblet was again lacking in beverage. She filled and drained it twice over before just grabbing the decanter from the servant and replenishing her drink herself, the bottle well hidden beneath the tablecloth between each pour.

By the time the container was dry, Flora didn't

mind. The alcohol was rapidly covering her with a warm blanket of haziness. The music was smoother, the dancers more animated, and her burning soul saved by the cool wine.

But when she saw the maid plant a hefty kiss upon Jasper's lips, Flora feared she would be ill. She swallowed the bile that crept up her throat and stood in her seat, brushing off Gwen's inquisitive look. She tried to make a graceful exit from the room, but the hem of her gown was trapped beneath the leg of her chair and it took two heavy pulls before she got the lace trim free. Jasper was staring at her by the time she began her walk through the feasting hall and out toward privacy and fresh air.

Once the hall's doors were closed behind her, Flora took a long breath to steady her spinning head. The stone floor rose like the sea beneath her, threatening to pull her down. She palmed the wall and gripped the grooves between the rocks. It was a poor excuse for a handle, but she feared that if she didn't hold on to something, the carpet under her feet would swallow her up.

She stumbled to the next open door, gulping down deep breaths of cool air. She was in the family's sitting room and someone had left the windows open, allowing for a fresh breeze to pour in. She sat on her knees upon the settee under the largest window and leaned on the stone windowsill, her cheek pressed against the velvet drapery. It was soft against her skin, and she found it strangely comforting.

It was dark outside, with no moon to light the hills to the right, nor the cliffs on the left. She could only see the outlines of the mounds in the distance and pinpricks of the stars in the sky. She remembered when she was young, her mother used to say that each star was a dream and one would fall from the sky at night, floating into her room in order to give her sweet visions in her sleep. When she was very young, she would feign slumber, waiting for a ball of light to creep into her window, which she was sure to keep open every night. Her mother was so cross with her when she saw the glass panes wide open, letting the frigid winter air into her room. But she couldn't be angry once she heard why her daughter was constantly tired and with a cold that never ended.

Flora smiled at the memory. It seemed like a lifetime ago, her being so young and easy to fool. But wasn't that happening with Jasper? Her being fooled? He whispered sweet words to her in the empty halls with no one around, but wouldn't declare his pure affections to Conner, nor ask for her hand in marriage. She wondered if her younger sister was right and Jasper was merely toying with her emotions.

She sighed and tore her gaze from the heavens. She had her fill of the clean air, so she lay back on the couch and closed her eyes, trying to ward off the wild spinning that was slowly ebbing to dull waves. There was no certainty that the ache of nausea would ever subside, as she had never been so wildly drunk before, and she debated leaving Penelope and Drummond's wedding reception for good, retiring to her bed for an early night.

"Flora, are ye in here?" a voice asked from the

doorway into the darkened room.

She lifted her head and squinted, merely making out a tall and wide figure. Her heart picked up a lively tempo and fluttered against her breastbone. "Yes?"

"Are ye well, lass?"

"Jasper?" Flora wasn't sure if it was truly him; maybe she only hoped it would be. She brought her torso up and draped her skirt over her legs, still allowing for a peek of bare ankle to show. "Is it you?"

"No...it's me, Big Angus. The MacLeod asked me to come and see if ye were ill."

She sighed heavily and dropped back to the decorative pillows. "I'm all right, thank you."

"Did ye...should I get Jasper for ye?" He sounded unsure. She guessed he had seen the way the pair flirted, but she didn't wish to ask.

"No, I only thought it might be him," Flora whispered, feeling embarrassed that she had inadvertently showed her weakness to the man.

"Do ye need help to your chambers, then?"

"No, thank you, that won't be necessary. I'm only taking the air."

Big Angus cleared his throat and shifted a bit before nodding. "I'll be off. I wish ye a well evenin'."

Flora waved him off before clasping her hands to her chest, hoping to slow the dreaded thumps that pounded in her ears. She noticed that Big Angus didn't shut the door behind him when he left, but Flora couldn't bring herself to get up and close it. The clock to one side of the room let off a series of ringing dongs, signaling that the midnight hour had begun. She knew that meant the wedding party in the grand hall wouldn't end for a few more hours yet, and she didn't relish the thought.

Groaning, she pushed herself up, breathing in one final, deep breath of frigid air before shambling across the sitting room, her hands grazing the chairs as she went. She could hear wafts of merrymaking drifting through the corridor, and was content to stay hidden in the crooks of the stone, just outside the feasting hall. Flora leaned against the wall, bracing herself for the long walk up to her chambers.

A shrill giggle shot through the comforting din and Flora threw her hands over her ears in surprise. But that sensation turned sickening when she saw who let loose the hacking laugh that jarred her so. Jasper came from the feasting hall, the busty maid clinging to his arm. Flora crept back, deeper into the shadows.

"Ach, lass," he crooned in the same voice he used with Flora in the quiet moments they stole together. "Ye can no' flirt with me so."

"And why not?" The maid pouted.

"Because I'm workin' on my standin' with the MacLeod, ye ken?"

The maid ran a finger down Jasper's chest, stopping when she hit his belt. "Oh, he won't mind a bit if ye have some fun, as long as ye do your work. And we both know how good o' a *worker* ye are."

"No, no, lass. Leave it be, aye?"

"But what if I do no' want to?"

"No, Una, no' now."

Flora rolled her eyes, disgusted with the way the maid—apparently called Una—was draped over Jasper, when he was clearly rejecting her advances. She couldn't help but feel a bit smug, watching him brush off Una's clambering hands. Surely he did little more than flirt with the maid in the feasting hall in order to make Flora jealous. She made a mental note to never tell him his plan had worked.

"Just come up to my chambers a moment, Jasper?" Una begged. "A short, wee moment is all I ask ye."

Jasper chuckled and patted the maid on the bum. "A wee nightcap, perhaps? Just a drink to see me through the dark hours."

Flora let out an audible gasp of "No!" Her drunken voice was several octaves louder than the whisper she aimed for.

"Who's that, then?" Una called out, her hands balled on her wide hips.

Flora shrank farther into her corner, her palm over her mouth, and her blood running cold. If Jasper and his wench caught her in the corner, there's no telling what they would have thought. They might suspect her of spying! Of course, that's exactly what she had been doing, but she would die before admitting it.

"We'd best be off, Una," Jasper whispered.

"Still fancy a nightcap?" the maid giggled.

Flora heard a series of rustling, not unlike the sounds of her own dress when she held them up to climb the stairs.

"No' here, lass!" Jasper chucked. "There's time

enough, yet."

She listened as the pair made their exit, their steps growing dimmer and dimmer until she was left alone in silence.

Chapter Two

Letting out a deep breath, Flora slid down to the floor to sit within a nest of sky blue silk ruffles. She took several gasps of air, relieved at not being caught, yet still deeply wounded at Jasper running off with the maid. Although neither of them verbally admitted what they would do once they reached Una's bedroom, Flora wasn't such a prude that she didn't know what would occur.

Although it sickened her, her mind wandered to Jasper and his nocturnal ventures. She wondered if he would truly follow Una up to the servants' quarters, relieve her of her plain brown dress, and bed the maid while Flora sat downstairs. She imagined what it would feel like to lure Jasper into her own bed, welcome him with open arms, and see his broad shoulders flex as he disrobed. Flora would run her hands down his muscular arms and kiss the single long scar that dashed across his cheek. Yes, she would finally kiss him, something she had been yearning for since he first came to the castle more than three years before.

The more she thought on what she *would* do with Jasper, the more she thought of what he *was* doing with Una. *Una* would be the one he embraced and whispered to in the dark. *Una* would be the one running her worn servant's fingers through his fiery mane. And *Una* would be the one to whisper "good morning" when the first light broke. Flora would still be alone.

The emotions flooded over inside her chest, spilling out her eyes and streaming down her cheeks. Quiet sobs shook her shoulders and Flora cursed herself for drinking so much wine. The honeyed alcohol only made her more upset and she knew her face would be red and puffy when she arose from bed the next day. Still, she couldn't stop the tears, which only frustrated her more. All she wanted to do was go up to her chambers and hide beneath the bedding to cry in peace, but she felt positively rooted to the ground, unable to pull herself upright.

Damn the bloody wine.

"Oh, help!" Flora cried lowly, blotting her face with the hem of her skirt. "Someone please assist me! I want to get off the bloody floor!"

She paused, listening for the sound of hurried footsteps, but none came.

"Hello? Do help! The stones are freezing and my arse is cold!" She let out a choked giggle at her own words. They cut through the ugly sobs.

When no one answered her second call, Flora knew that all available servants would be in the feasting hall and no one would be wandering the corridors aimlessly. She also understood that she had to get up and make her way to her chambers before people began leaving the wedding feast. There was no way she would be caught dead completely inebriated and puffed, sitting in a ball in her crumpled silks.

Flora looked about and caught sight of a tall candelabra to her right. It wasn't lit, so she grasped onto the black iron and counted to three in her mind before attempting to hoist herself upward. She immediately fell back, the candleholder crashing to the stones below with a defining crack.

Not able to handle the sheer ridiculousness, Flora began laughing so hard, her sides were torn in two and fresh waves of tears formed in her eyes.

"Madam?" a voice questioned. "Are you well?"

She opened her eyes and looked up, seeing the tall figure of Andrew Philips standing over her, his lips pressed into a thin line. "Mr. Philips. Fancy meeting you in the hallway."

"Are you hurt?" he asked her seriously. "Shall I fetch someone?"

Flora paused, confused. Was she speaking to the same Andrew Philips with the terrible speech impediment? This voice was clear and deep, a crisp sound in the quiet. "Mr. Philips? *Andrew* Philips? From London? The one studying law?"

"The very same."

Not entirely convinced, she asked, "Do you promise?"

"Yes. Might I help you up?" He held out a hand, but Flora kept her own upon her lap. She was entirely too stunned to move.

"Why, Mr. Philips, your stutter…you're *cured*!"

He raised his brows and the corners of his lips twitched. "Right, yes. Let's get you up now, Madam."

Flora allowed him to take her hands and pull her up. The sudden movements made her head spin. She grasped Andrew's arm, but he didn't move, making him the perfect crutch. She patted him on the shoulder appreciatively. "Goodness, you're a sturdy fellow."

"Thank you, Madam." He looked around the empty corridor. "Shall I fetch someone to take you back to your quarters?"

"No! No one must see me so...so..." She searched for words that could fully explain how terrible she looked. Swollen? Bloodshot? Disheveled? Messy?

"Drunk?" Andrew offered helpfully.

"Yes, Mr. Philips. I'm so terribly drunk and I don't wish anyone to see me in such a state."

She watched as Andrew's head swiveled about, seemingly looking for something. "Well, I suppose I could escort you to your chambers..."

"Smashing!" Flora began pulling him toward the stairs, but faltered, the tip of her slipper tripping on air. Luckily, Andrew had a firm grasp on her hand and threw the other about her waist to steady her.

"Are you all right?"

"A little wobbly, truth be told." She abruptly felt tired—so very, *very* tired. The events of the evening had drained her. "I think I must sleep now." She began letting her legs grow limp, and she wanted nothing more that to rest right where she stood. "I'll be fine here."

"No, no, Madam. We must go on," Andrew told her firmly, struggling to keep her upright at she fought to be let down to sleep.

"No, thank you," Flora mumbled as her knees hit the stone.

Then she was swung up in the air and into Andrew's arms. She knew she wasn't a particularly heavy woman, but she still wouldn't have expected him to be able to lift her. Still, his grasp was rather comfortable and she leaned her head upon his shoulder, which felt much more defined and muscular than she would have thought.

"Now, Madam, please tell me where your chambers are."

Flora racked her brain, her thoughts melting together. "Up the stairs."

"How many stairs?"

"One flight," she replied thoughtfully. "Perhaps two? You won't drop me?"

"I certainly hope not."

They began their arduous journey, strolling through the sitting room and to the narrow family staircase that led to her private quarters. As he began the climb, Flora threw her arms about his neck, frightened at being released to fall to her death. She had fallen down those same steps as a child, and still had the scar on her chin to show for it. She could feel Andrew's steady heartbeat against her fingers, and that calmed her a bit. So she closed her eyes and took deep breaths. She could smell him—a faint scent of lemon and something else she couldn't identify. It was almost the same aroma that came from some of Conner's older library books.

"Is this your floor, Madam?"

Flora opened her eyes, thankful to be closer to the comforts of her own bed. "Aye. Second door."

Andrew nodded and walked her to the door before placing her carefully upon her feet, one hand at her elbow to help her stay upright. "Now shall I call for a maid?"

"No, I'll be all right. Thank you, Mr. Philips," she whispered, breaking his hold on her and seizing the knob. "I never could have done it without you."

"Quite all right, Madam."

Flora waved her free hand. "Please, don't call me Madam. I'm only nineteen. Call someone else Madam."

"As you wish." He bobbed a short bow. "Good evening, Miss MacLeod."

"Good evening, Mr. Philips. Top notch carrying skills." Flora gave him a pat on the arm before going into her room and locking the door behind her.

She almost debated pulling the cord for a maid, but didn't need any gossip concerning her obnoxious inebriation in the kitchens. Instead, she stomped to her bed, kicking off her slippers and pulling at the back of her gown, trying to reach the fastenings. Flora managed to get a few unhooked and pulled the gown over her head. Finally, she sloppily unlaced enough of her corset to shimmy out of it.

Her sheets were deliciously cool to the touch and felt wonderful against her hot skin. She was about to slip into sleep when she had a thought. Although silly, she felt as if she needed to open her window—

to let a falling star bring a dream, as her mother used to say. With all the unhappiness her love of Jasper had brought her, Flora felt as if she needed a dream that night.

Groaning, she pushed herself off her bed and wobbled toward one of her narrow windows, using a chair and a small writing desk to aid in her venture. Heaving deep breaths, pushing the window open was harder than she remembered. Another final thrust opened the glass, letting the early fall air rush in.

She wanted to stay by the window a bit longer, to take in the salt air coming up from the cliffs, but Flora knew she desperately needed rest. She shuffled back to her four-poster and slid beneath the down comforter. With each moment, her body relaxed and the fresh breeze caressed her skin. Flora watched the night sky, where the stars were slowly disappearing with the pink early morning light that threatened to spill over the horizon.

The sunrise was coming, breaking a new day that Flora didn't anticipate. Her mind was awash with images of Jasper and the maid. The drunken thoughts weren't kind and Flora begged them to leave so she could sleep. The idea of seeing Jasper on the castle grounds wasn't a pleasant one. She knew she would only imagine him coming from Una's bed and there was no telling when she would again see the maid again; certainly at the next large family meal.

Flora turned over, her back to the window. The stars were all gone, and so were the dreams she once had.

Chapter Three

Flora slowly opened her eyes; the bright morning light streaming in from the open window nearly blinded her. She threw her arm over her face and groaned. The events of the night before washed over her, more biting than the sun. She lay in a puddle of embarrassment, shame, and pain from a pounding headache.

She reached up and knocked on the paneling above her headboard. Her aim was to get her little sister's attention, as their beds shared a wall, an almost makeshift one at that. While most of the partitions in the castle were stone, this single one was made of wood, as their separate dwellings were once one. Ever since childhood, they communicated with raps upon the paneling. But that morning there was no secret message, only the desperate call of the hung-over.

After a dozen knocks, Gwen bounced in. "Yes?"

"Gwen," Flora rasped, peeking out from under her arm. "I feel I might die. You must write my will and testament. Your handwriting is so much neater than mine."

"You're not going to die. You merely smell like a brewery and look even worse." She crinkled her small nose delicately.

"You have the most soothing voice, I can almost ignore the nastiness of your statement." She closed her eyes again.

"Shall I fetch you something?"

Flora felt the bed shift and knew Gwen had sat down near her feet. "A quicker death."

"So dramatic. Tell me, what happened last night? One moment you were guzzling wedding wine, and the next, you were gone. Big Angus said he saw you lying in the sitting room, but you had disappeared by the time I came to find you."

"I can't recall. It's too shameful."

"I'm sure it's not all that bad."

Flora rolled over to put her back to the windows and peered at Gwen through lowered lashes. "I saw Jasper."

Gwen pursed her lips. "So did everyone."

"I saw him with…with…"

"With whom?"

"A maid called Una." She tried to brush the image of their embrace from her mind. It made her feel sick. "They were pawing at one another and she…they…oh, Gwen." She began to cry, although she didn't wish to.

Gwen crawled up next to Flora and lay down beside her, taking her hand. "I'm sorry, that's just monstrous. He's such a filthy cad."

"I just can't believe what I saw," she sniffed, wiping at her eyes. "He made such a show of refusing to dance with me that I kept drinking. Then I was so ill with drink, I could barely stand up. And I was all alone in the hallway, trapped on the floor."

"Than how did you get to bed?"

Flora sighed. She had almost forgotten her little adventure with the British man. "I nearly forgot that part, although I sincerely wish I had."

"What?"

"Do you know Andrew Philips?"

Gwen's brow furrowed as she thought. "Is he rather tall and handsome? Dark red hair?"

"The same," Flora confirmed. "It's a bit blurry, but I think he found me in the corridor outside the feasting hall and was forced to...to carry me upstairs."

Gwen's pale cheeks pinked. "Certainly he did not!"

"He did."

"Goodness, that is improper. I'm glad no one saw. If someone had, everyone would know about it by now."

"I don't know if it's the drink or the humiliation that will send me to an early grave."

"Flora, the only place you're being sent right now is the bath."

The mere thought of rising from her soft, down pillows made nauseous. "Must I?"

"I insist."

Flora watched as Gwen rose from the bed and crossed to the bathroom. She could hear the water begin filling the porcelain tub. Little Gwendolyn had always been a miniature nurse, which was always odd, considering she was the youngest of the

30

MacLeod flock. If any of the girls or Conner were ill, Gwen would be the one to feed them broth and pour them tea, imploring them to stay abed. Flora thought that if she hadn't been a noble born lady, Gwen would have certainly trained as a healer.

When Gwen left the bathroom to fetch Flora, her golden curls had been hastily pinned up at the top of her head. "Now, let's get you up."

"Can't I just wallow for a bit? At least until the afternoon?"

"It *is* noon, Flora," Gwen told her with her hands upon her hips. "We're going to get you cleaned up, dressed, and downstairs for luncheon with the rest of the guests."

"I can't do it." She pulled the covers over her head and nestled deeper into the mattress, willing her sister to let her die in peace.

The blankets were abruptly torn from Flora's body, leaving her chilled. "Gwendolyn, I declare, you may be the slightest of all our sisters, but you're certainly the strongest."

"Up, up, *up*!"

Flora's skull throbbed with each word. "I'll rise if you'll be quiet for a moment."

Gwen nodded and crossed her arms, her small foot tapping on the stone.

The floor was cold under Flora's feet and she hurried to the tub. The comforting scent of violet and eucalyptus greeted her and seemed to heal some of her headache. She hurried out of her shift and into the warm, murky water. Flora held her hair atop her head and sunk deeper until her shoulders were submerged.

Gwen entered, several hairpins in her fist. She sat on the edge of the tub and her fingers made quick work of Flora's hair. No tendril was left to dangle.

"I've always loved your hair," Gwen whispered, tucking the last strand behind Flora's ear. "It's like strands of spun gold."

"Yours is just as nice."

"The color, yes, but my curls get all in a tangle while yours hangs straight and soft." She picked up a squat green container and held it out to Flora. "Guess what I have?"

"When did we get eucalyptus scents? I thought we used it all months ago." Flora had missed the foreign, minty smell.

"Conner had them brought in a few days ago when a ship came with some of the things for Penelope and Drum's wedding."

"Which ship? Was it the Portuguese trader?"

Gwen shrugged. "Perhaps. There's all manner of queer objects in the larder now. I was looking for the books Conner promised me when I found the new bottle."

"Thank you for bringing it."

"I'm going to go lay out a gown," Gwen told her, rising from her perch. "Do try not to drown. I'm much too busy to be pulling you from a watery grave at present."

Flora rolled her eyes and rested in the fragrant water, which was rapidly cooling by the minute. She knew she would soon be forced from its comforting warmth, but couldn't bear the reality of it. Leaving that bath was the first step toward rejoining the busy household below. She couldn't stomach the thought of seeing Jasper again in the halls or being served tea by busty Una. She couldn't touch a single teacake served by the woman, knowing where her hands had been. It was enough to make her stomach twist into knots.

Not able to stew in her own thoughts a moment more, she grabbed the towel Gwen had left and climbed out of the tub, hurriedly wrapping herself. Once she had dried, she went into her bedroom, where Gwen sat at her dressing table, smelling her perfume bottles.

"Your clothes are all on the bed."

Flora shuffled to where her gown and underthings were laid out and hastily pulled them on, calling Gwen over when it came time to button the soft green velvet in the back. She didn't bother with jewels, or dressing her hair much more than running a brush through the long locks. The mere idea of having her hair pinned up into the tight curls and coils as she did in London would do nothing to help her splitting headache.

She linked arms with Gwen and allowed her sister to lead her downstairs and into the feasting hall, where all the wedding guests were breaking their fast…or rather, partaking in an afternoon meal. She had forgotten how many people had stayed in the castle and the hall was nearly as busy as it had been the night before. Thankfully, it wasn't as loud.

As they walked between the tables to the head seats at the front of the room, Flora locked eyes with Jasper. He sat among his friends and shot her a cheeky grin as she passed, as he usually had every day past for almost two years. Normally, the small look would hearten her, but that day it felt like a cannonball to the chest. He was acting as if he hadn't slighted her at the wedding feast, nor followed Una up to her chambers afterward. It was disgusting.

She turned her nose up at him and straightened her back, trying to send a clear message that he had fallen out of her good graces. Another also caught her gaze. Andrew Philips sat at the end of one table, taking nothing but tea. He held a small book in his hand, and most notably, had a pair of round spectacles balanced upon his straight nose. Flora thought it a most unusual sight, as almost no one wore glasses in their part of the highlands.

He was still reading when Flora sat at her place between Conner and Gwen. She wondered briefly what book was so interesting it had to come with him to dine. But Conner's curious gaze brought her out of her musing.

"What is my wee sister starin' at?" Conner asked, passing his infant son Alec to a nursemaid.

Flora looked down as a servant—thankfully not Una—placed sandwiches and fruit upon her plate. "Nothing."

"Conner, you leave your sister alone or I swear I'll stab you in the hand with my fork!" Charlotte threatened from his other side.

"Ach, ye jest. Ye'd never harm my hands. Ye love them! Just last night you told me how ye like when I—"

Thunk.

Flora's head shot up to see Conner cradling his

34

right hand, his mouth gaping open, staring at his wife. "You *stabbed* me, ye daft lass!"

"Merely a graze," Charlotte corrected calmly. "A warning shot, if you will."

Flora leaned over, seeing the faintest of scratches on the back of Conner's hand, right below his knuckles. "You're so dramatic. There isn't even any blood."

"I could have died," Conner asserted seriously. "This will scar, I'm sure of it."

"Good thing I like scars then." Charlotte smiled sweetly and offered her husband a slice of orange, which he gladly took before leaning in to whisper in her ear, making the woman glow pink.

"Ugh, sickening," Flora grumbled, biting into her sandwich. Although she didn't understand their odd dynamic, she knew they were happy. Seeing Conner and Charlotte so revoltingly in love made her own loss sting all the more.

"Don't be jealous," chastised Gwen quietly. "You're already wearing a green dress, you needn't add more of the hue to your person."

Flora huffed. Gwen was right, she *was* jealous, and it didn't suit her. It was all well and good when she was staying in London, going to balls and dancing with men and allowing them to take her to the theater. She had nary given Jasper another thought when soft British men in England were pursuing her. Not even in the wee morning moments had she overly worried about the Scot. But with him so near, she felt herself drawn to him in an unhealthy manner, pushing away all others, even when he hurt her so.

"I think I'm going to go take the air," Flora told Gwen as she pushed away her half finished food. "I need to clear my head."

"Want me to come with you?"

She shook her head. "No. I just need to think."

As Flora strolled along the side of the hall, taking care to stay far away from Jasper's table, someone calling her name stopped her. Andrew Philips was approaching, tucking his glasses into the front pocket of his morning coat.

"Good day, Miss MacLeod," he said with a nod.

She blanched as she recalled him carrying her inebriated body up to her chambers. The feelings of sheer mortification rose up her chest and settled into her cheeks. "Hello, Mr. Philips. About last night—"

He held up a hand. "Please, say nothing of it, for both our sakes."

"But I must thank you for your help…and your *discretion*."

It was Andrew's turn to flush, but he turned his face down to look at his timepiece. "Please, say no more. Might I escort you anywhere? I'm on my way to meet my carriage at present. I must catch the evening train."

"No, thank you. I was just going for a walk around the grounds. I'll come with you as far as the main door, though."

He held out his arm, which she gratefully took. The look of pure shock on Jasper's face in the corner of her eye made her draw the Englishman all the closer as they left the feasting hall. She hoped that Jasper felt a sliver of the pain he had inflicted upon her the night before.

"Mr. Philips, what was the book I saw you reading just now?"

"Well, um…" He cleared his throat before drawing it out of his pocket with a free hand. It was a soft yellow leather, black letters spelled out *Songs and Legends of the MacLeod Clan.* "I picked this up in one of the shops in Edinburg before coming north. I wanted to learn a bit about the area and this is all I could find on your household."

Flora plucked the book from his hand. "Do you know who wrote this?"

"No, I didn't think to look."

"Drummond MacGregor." Flora laughed. "Penelope's husband!"

His dark eyes glimmered jovially. "My word, you don't say!"

She flipped open the cover, showing him Drum's name. "It is. He released it almost directly after the first." Flora then gave the book back to him, watching as he brushed his thumb over the embossed words on the front before slipping it back into his jacket.

"I do wish I knew this before. I really must tell him how much I enjoy his work next time I see him with the Elmslys in London."

When they reached the main door, a manservant passed Andrew his hat. He released Flora from his arm and popped the hat on his head before turning back to her.

"Well, Miss MacLeod, it's been…quite entertaining."

"It has," she agreed, glad he wasn't about to tease her, although she would have deserved it for how drunk she was in his presence.

"I suppose I must get to my carriage," he said, but made no move to do so.

Flora bit her lip, feeling oddly like a specimen under a microscope as he regarded her with his warm brown gaze. "I hope you have a pleasant journey."

"Miss MacLeod, will you be coming to London any time in the future?"

"I can't say at present. I've only just returned home."

"Certainly…certainly. Well, it was lovely meeting you, Miss MacLeod. Goodbye."

"Goodbye," she replied.

Flora watched Andrew reach his carriage. He turned to glance at her once more before disappearing within and beginning his travel toward home. She felt almost sorry to see him go. He had quite opened up in their short hours together, although she was still wildly curious as to where his abominable stutter had come from and where it had gone so suddenly. His true voice was a comfortable baritone, his words the fine, melodic clip of an English gentleman.

"Flora," another voice rumbled at her side.

She glanced up to see Jasper standing over her, his eyes wild. He seemed angry with her and her heart began pounding as he loomed over her. He wouldn't ever hurt her, physically at least, but his irate presence unsettled her.

"Jasper," she greeted shortly before beginning her walk at a swift pace. Although it was unladylike, she hoped to outrun him, but his legs were much longer than hers. She made it out the gate and into the open land before he grabbed her arm.

"Flora," he growled again.

She pulled away and planted her hands on her hips. "Flora, Flora, *Flora*! Don't you have anything else to say?"

His brows rose, all former anger gone from his features. "Flora, are ye cross with me?"

"Oh, do I have a reason to be?" she asked sarcastically.

He shrugged his broad shoulders. "No, I do no' think so. I only spied ye with that Brit and wanted to see what ye were up to."

"We were just talking, not that it is any of *your* business." She stalked away, her shoes sinking into the tufts of grass beneath them.

He jogged slightly to keep up with her hurried strides. "Flora, speak to me, I beg ye."

"Go away, Jasper." She felt hot tears prick the backs of her eyelids, but she was resolute that she would drop dead before letting him see her fall to pieces.

"Flora, what's wrong?"

Exasperated, she stopped and turned on him. "You! *You're* what's wrong! I saw you in the bloody hall with that bloody maid, and again later, letting her lead you to her room! I was *there*, Jasper! You said all the pretty words *I* longed to hear, yet bedded some scullery girl!"

He rubbed at the back of his neck, gazing down at the ground. "Ach, lass…it's no' what ye think."

"I'm young, Jasper, not a total fool."

"I never said ye were." He took her hands in hers, and although she hated to admit it, the feeling of their sturdy roughness helped to soothe her wounded heart.

"You made a fool out of me," she admitted quietly, her words almost whipped away by the highland winds. "I've tried so hard, but you cast me aside to bed another without a thought to me."

"Flora...Flora, it's only been you. O' course I flirt a bit with some o' the lasses, but only because I dare no' touch ye."

"What do you mean? You're touching me now."

"Ye are the laird's sister. I only want you, but I dare no' act on my feelin's. I respect ye and the MacLeod too much. I only flirt with the others so the lads do no' torment me. I never mean to hurt ye and I will no'. I did no'...*bed* Una. I only made it look so...for the lads, ye see? There's only you, Flora."

Her breath hitched in her throat and she struggled to control the sea of confusing emotions whirling within her. On one hand, she wished nothing more than to slap him across his handsome face. On the other, falling into his arms would feel heavenly. Jasper had finally said all the things she longed to hear. He admitted she was the one for him and confessed that he *hadn't* bedded Una. Still, he had wounded her pride and made her doubt all his previous whispers of love...well, caring, as he had never said explicitly that he loved her.

Despite her tumultuous feelings, her heart won over her mind and she collapsed into his chest, allowing herself to cry into the rough fabric of his weathered plaid. He patted her back and leaned his cheek atop her head. It felt ever so intimate and Flora despised the thought of ever pulling away, although Jasper did first.

"There's a storm comin'. I feel the winds change," he murmured. "Let's get back inside before the rain starts."

"Jasper," she began, her voice wavering. "Do you mean to make your intentions clear to my brother?"

He frowned. "My intentions?"

"Yes, he'll want to know that you'll be able to care for me…and any children."

He scratched his chin, his eyes trained on the gray sky. "Oh, that. Aye, aye, I will."

Flora felt as if her heart would leap from her chest, it was so light. The weight of keeping their romance a secret for so long and having the burden lifted from her soul was invigorating. The possibility of having Jasper as her husband was brilliant and she wanted nothing more than to go to Conner that very moment to make their relationship known. Then Jasper would no longer have to toy with the maids to keep his friends from teasing him. It was perfect. But she wasn't about to let his fake dalliance with Una go so easily.

"I'll have you know I'm still miffed about your entanglement with Una, no matter how false, and I'm not about to forgive so easily."

Jasper's cheeky grin from earlier had returned. "Aye? Then what should I do to beg your forgiveness?"

"That's up to you to decide," she told him

shortly before beginning a leisurely stroll back to the castle.

Her steps were significantly lighter. Flora was pleased that Jasper had admitted his thoughts on a potential marriage and that they were able to resume their normal flirtations in public. Perhaps they could be handfasted on the morrow, making them able to relish the joys of marriage while still planning a large wedding for the spring. She knew she couldn't outlast the months ahead.

"I think I know how to get ye to forgive me," Jasper called, matching her steps.

"Oh, have you? And how's that?" she asked with a smile.

"With a kiss."

"A kiss?"

"Aye. Just a wee one to keep between you and I."

They stood together before the walls of the MacLeod keep, their eyes locked. Flora felt her knees grow weak as he moved closer. Jasper cupped one cheek and leaned down, pausing a moment before pressing his lips to hers in the briefest caress—so swift, Flora wouldn't have known it even happened, if it did not leave a touch of fire in its wake.

"Just a kiss," Jasper crooned, his fingertips brushing Flora's jawbone. "Just a wee kiss."

Chapter Four

Three days had passed quietly since Flora's kiss with Jasper. While she had left their meeting feeling as if all was falling into place, he proved her wrong. When she sent word to meet her in the family sitting room after supper to speak with Conner about the handfasting, Jasper never arrived. Flora was left sitting in silence, pretending to read the same page in her book, her eyes constantly flitting toward the door and her heart leaping into her throat at each passing sound of footsteps. When the hour grew late and the fire had burned almost to embers, it was clear Jasper was not coming.

She was left to stew in her anger, the dull flame heating her chest. Flora was pleased when the Elmslys left, taking Matthew with them. The lack of male companionship allowed her to convene with Charlie over the matter of her absent intended. Charlie always had a knack for the matters of men, both in the boardroom and the bedroom, and she was sure he would show her the way.

Charlie sat in his dressing robe, a pipe in his lips,

when Flora came to his guest chambers. Normally, it would be rather unseemly to be alone with a man, but Charlie's true interests were a well-accepted "secret." So Flora was quite content to sit with him before the fire, eating candied plums and getting unbiased opinions on the matter of her almost engagement.

"Darling, I've met men like him," Charlie told her in a confident manner. "I've *been* a man like him. I'm not certain he has any interest in pursuing anything further."

"But he says differently," Flora replied, feeling a tad miffed that the first words out of Charlie's lips branded Jasper a cad.

He patted her hand. "I know, I know. That's the way of men. They whisper pretty things then do another. It's not fair, but it's just in their—*our* nature."

"Well, at least you never lie to me."

"And I won't. Now, tell me what it is you truly want with Jasper. I understand your attraction…everyone can see he's rather good-looking in that rugged and outdoorsy sense, but is he truly husband material?"

"Everything thinks not," Flora admitted. "But I see him differently. He takes such care when he's with me and tells me he wants only me in his life."

"Flora, have you…" Charlie's gaze darted toward the closed door and his voice lowered. "Well, have you taken him to your bed?"

Her cheeks flamed. "Certainly not. I intend to be his wife first. He says…well, he's always been quite pleased at me staying pure for him."

He chuckled, his mouth full of plums. "Forgive me, you just wouldn't be the first around here who has taken a ride on the Highland Express in order to get their man."

"You're terrible!" Flora laughed. "But I haven't, nor has Jasper pressured me to do so. He's never once behaved inappropriately."

"That does change things, doesn't it?" he muttered, almost to himself.

"How so?"

"You said that this flirtation has lasted the better part of two years, yes?"

"Around that."

"Two years and only a *single kiss* to show for it." Charlie chewed the end of his unlit pipe and sighed. "I'm not sure if I should be sad for you or pat you on the back for keeping your petticoats down."

"What do you mean? Why would you feel sad for me?"

"You see, darling, when a man is besotted with a woman mind, body, and soul, he can almost never control his desire."

"You mean like Charlotte and Conner?"

"Precisely. Now look at Penelope and her old beau Theodore. She told us herself that their relationship had no passion even before she found him...handling the help. Now, between her and that Drummond...well, one might say that their longing is what brought them to the altar."

"But they do love each other."

"Yes, yes, but you're missing the point. What do both Charlotte and Penelope have in common when it comes to getting married?"

Flora paused. Of course there was love in both couplings, but there was more that that—a tangible spark everyone noticed whenever they came into a room. There was an aura about them and each moved in perfect alignment to one another. And there was another thing…both pairings were physically drawn to one another to the point of nauseating all who came to view them.

"I suppose they are all very physically connected."

"And were so *before* marriage."

"Oh…well…" Flora floundered. That thought hadn't even crossed her mind. "Surely you aren't suggesting I take Jasper into my bed?"

Charlie let out a deep, bellowing laugh. "Goodness no, you daft little lamb."

She let out a breath of relief. "I'm pleased to hear it."

"That wouldn't help things in the slightest. If he's been avoiding you for days, I wouldn't think that would be in your best interest."

"Do you think it's a lost cause?" Flora asked, feeling her heart sink. "Have I wasted my youth?"

"Wasted your youth? Darling Flora, you're only just at the cusp of your youth. Of course I don't mean to minimize your feelings, but pining over that scoundrel in your adolescence and being betrayed doesn't mean you're destined to be a spinster."

"A spinster," she said, a loveless future looming menacingly over her.

"Don't fret about spinsterhood," Charlie commanded stoutly. "I won't let it come to that."

"Oh? What would you do then? Force Jasper to marry me?"

"Don't be a fool. I'll do it myself."

A strangled sound akin to a chuckle burst from her lips. "Certainly you're joking?"

"Not at all," he replied evenly, packing another pinch of tobacco into his pipe. "I think it would be a rather good arrangement for the both of us. You could be free to do as you wished and visit me in London at your pleasure. Meanwhile, I could pursue my own interests while appeasing society at large. Our combined fortunes would leave us living a comfortable life and we're already such good friends. I see it as a comfortable end, if you find yourself without a man."

Flora giggled. "No offense, Charlie, but I had hoped to marry for love, not freedom."

He shrugged and leaned back into his armchair. "Suit yourself. I'll just have to marry some other charming lady who doesn't mind me dallying with her brothers and uncles."

"I wish you all the luck in the world."

"It won't be too hard. I'll just find a woman who also finds no pleasure in the company of the other sex."

Flora contemplated his words for a brief moment before her jaw fell open. "Do you mean to say there are women who enjoy the company of other women...*intimately*?"

"My sweet summer child." Charlie grinned and looked toward the fire. "You do have much to learn about the world."

***

Flora left her conversation with Charlie even more confused than before. But she had learned many things; the most notable being that Charlie would be her backup husband, saving her from an empty life of spinsterhood, and the other being that some women didn't have any interest in men at all. Jolly good for them, she'd say, as they were free from the endless lies men spout.

Not wishing to go to her room, she wandered aimlessly down the corridors and found herself before the empty feasting hall. Her gentle footfalls hardly made a sound against the stone. As she sat on one of the worn wooden benches, Flora could hear the distant dim of the servants preparing supper in the kitchens below. So much life teamed within the castle, but she often felt so very alone. She laid her head atop her arms on the tabletops and prepared to have good cry.

"Flora?" asked a rough voice behind her.

She lifted her head and saw Jasper standing in the doorway of the hall. "What are you doing here?"

"I was lookin' for ye," he answered, taking steady steps in her direction.

"Is that so?" she shot back with more venom in her voice than she would have liked. Flora hated the thought of him seeing her as anything other than a perfectly poised lady of breeding.

"Aye."

"Well, that's surprising, as I believe you've been hiding from me."

"Ach, no. I'd never hide from ye."

"You're a terrible liar."

Jasper rubbed the back of his neck, his gaze traveling about the room, anywhere but toward her face. "Well, I did no' hide from ye…"

"Then what were you doing?"

"I was merely bidin' my time."

Flora tried to swallow her anger, but his avoidance of her statements was making it almost impossible to do. "Jasper, if you have nothing of value to say, then leave me be."

"Lass, do no' be vexed with me," he muttered, grabbing one of her hands and holding it tightly between his own.

She debated pulling her fingers from his grasp, but found that she enjoyed his touch too much. "And why shouldn't I be? You've been completely avoiding me. You didn't even come when I summoned you to speak with Conner!"

"Ah, aye. Well, ye see…I could no' come."

"And why ever not? The cattle have all been brought in from the hills for winter, there are no feuds, and all the taxes have been collected. What matter was so pressing that you couldn't even send word to me?" She drew away from him and angled her body toward the far wall, her back to him. "I waited in that study for *hours*, Jasper. I was humiliated."

"And I'm sorry, Flora. I never meant to harm ye."

"Then what did you mean to do?" She felt hot tears well in her eyes, but she tried to keep her composure. She couldn't let him see her weak and in pain.

49

"I…I was just…the MacLeod never would allow it. There's no way he would ever allow it."

Flora felt the weight of his hand press down upon her shoulder. She shrugged it off. "How would you know? You weren't even brave enough to speak with him."

"Because I know him. I've fought with him. I've shared his home and drank from his cup. He respects me as a man, but would never think me good enough for his sister."

"You didn't even try."

"He'd have me flogged."

Flora whipped around to face him. "He would never! Not if he knew that you would treat me well."

"He'd never trust me with ye."

She studied his face, so ruggedly cut and earnest, and almost believed him. Conner could be judgmental and suspicious, almost to a fault. But, then again, that's how he held his seat as Laird. "He just thinks me too young and foolish to make decisions for myself."

"*I* do no' think ye young and foolish," Jasper told her fervently.

"I'm tired of him brushing away my feelings and you being too frightened to act upon them."

"Flora, I—"

"No!" She stood, her skirts flying around her ankles. "No more excuses and no more fearful, pathetic justifications!"

A pained look flashed upon Jasper's features, but he made no moves to calm her. "Please, Flora."

She held up her hand. "Don't. Just…don't."

Flora stalked from the feasting hall. When she reached the main corridor, she paused, waiting for the heavy thuds of booted feet, but Jasper didn't follow her. And she had the dreaded feeling he never would.

***

Flora locked herself in her chambers. She felt frustrated beyond belief and horribly disheartened. She had held a small candle of hope for a marriage with Jasper, but the last of that hope had been dashed, leaving her in the dark. Her future now looked dimmer than ever, her dream of a life with Jasper further from her grasp than ever before. And it was all because of Conner.

In a fit of childish rage, she pushed the stack of mystery novels from her nightstand. They fell to the floor in a series of satisfied thumps, some of their pages flying out and scattering about the room. Conner had bought her those books, the dress she wore, the slippers on her feet, the fragrant soap she bathed in. Did that mean he felt he bought and owned *her*? Is that why he denied her at every turn?

She threw open her wardrobe and drug out her silk gowns and fur stoles, tossing them to the ground. Next came her chessboard with the ivory pieces. Conner had given the set to Flora for her birthday and she had been so pleased to receive it. Now it was nothing more than another reminder that Conner owned her.

"Not anymore," she cried, overturning the small table it sat upon, scattering pawns and knights across the room.

Her chambers were in shambles, her belongings torn from their places. And Flora didn't care a bit. Everything she owned, everything she was, resulted from the control her blasted brother had over her. He dominated every facet of her life from what gown she wore to the education she received. Now he planned on controlling who she would spend her life with! Flora wouldn't stand for such vile injustices. But how could she marry for love against all Conner's wishes?

Conner had married Charlotte when she escaped from the clutches of a brutish forced marriage. Without her father's permission, Conner had taken Charlotte to wife. And as for her cousin Drummond, he had gotten himself Penelope when the pair consummated their love out of wedlock. Penelope had forced her parents' hand by the loss of her virginity and now she was on her honeymoon with the man she loved. But what could Flora do? Jasper lived in Scotland, so there was no running away with him.

"What do I do now?" she muttered, stepping over the piles of clothes and flopping onto her bed.

Surely she couldn't do what Penelope and Drummond did—lie together without at least a handfasting to bind them. But were there any other options? Anything other than bedding Jasper to force Conner to accept the match? Then again, would there be any true harm in lying with Jasper? After all, they would be married directly after telling Conner.

Flora laid on her stomach, twirling a lock of hair

around one finger. All she needed to do in order to cement her future was seduce the man she loved. One night of sinful passion could lead to a lifetime of wedded bliss!

Chapter Five

"You're going to do *what*?" Charlie hissed, choking on his brandy.

"I'm going to 'do a Penelope,' as it were," Flora whispered excitedly in their secluded corner of her chambers the next afternoon. "Think of it: If I'm properly bedded and possibly carrying a child out of wedlock, Conner will have no choice but marry me to Jasper in order to save my reputation."

"Do you really think that wise?"

"Wiser than marrying *you*, that's for certain."

Charlie shrugged and put down his empty cup before turning toward her, his face drawn and tight. "Flora, you know I thoroughly enjoy a good scandal, but normally not one that could backfire so spectacularly on those I love."

"Truly, I don't see the downside."

"What if your brother still doesn't allow you to wed him?"

"And leave me potentially pregnant out of wedlock? Hardly possible."

"I suppose you do have a point. After all, our

dear Penelope was almost shoved down the aisle by her parents to hide any potential pregnancy." Charlie chuckled. "But how will you complete your little plot? It's not as if your Jasper can just traipse into your bedchamber in plain sight. He's not *me*."

"I thought I'd go to his."

"He lives here in the castle?"

"Yes. Most men who serve under Conner do if there's room enough, or they have to care for their farms. Him being unattached means he's free to room in the outer wings of the keep. I believe he even has his own room since Big Angus left to ready his farm for his own wedding."

"So Jasper owns no land?"

"Oh, I didn't say that. He has some spinster aunt who lives on his farm some miles away. She oversees things with the help of some lad, I believe."

"Then your plan is just sashay into his chambers and under his kilt?"

Flora nibbled her bottom lip and slouched deeper into her seat. "I…I don't know. I mean…what do I *do*? I've never done anything like this."

"How *delicious*," Charlie muttered. His mouth split open into a toothy grin and he tapped his fingers together. "I am to be an accessory to a wondrous plot."

"Don't call it a plot. Now tell me what I am to do."

"If you haven't noticed, I do not have the necessary parts for your endeavor," he pointed out, motioning to his lap.

"Come now, Charlie, you're the only man I trust

to help."

He breathed deeply through his nose and looked around the room. "I suppose I could be of some assistance. Besides, I had a great deal of fun at Penelope's wedding, so you getting married would give me an excuse to dally in Scotland for a while longer."

Charlie rose from his chair and began pacing Flora's—now clean—room. He poked about her dresser full of gowns and inspected her dressing table. She watched him intently as he sniffed her perfume bottles and grimaced at each.

"What are you doing?" she asked as he tossed aside one particularly large bottle.

"Trying to help you. You need to be alluring this evening."

Flora's stomach dropped. "Should it be so soon?"

"How much longer should you wait?"

"I suppose you're right. Now help me, Charlie. Make me irresistible."

He placed a hand over his heart. "Oh, darling, I thought you'd never ask."

***

"I feel foolish," Flora grumbled as Charlie finished dabbing bright pats of red lip color to her mouth.

"Well, you don't look foolish, and that's all that matters."

She clutched her black cloak tighter around her chest. Charlie had forced her out of her gown and stays, leaving her in naught but a thin shift. He had then piled her hair atop her head in a wild fashion, leaving her looking "freshly bedded," as he called it. Rouge and lip color followed, as did several dabs of a musky rose scent to her neck. While he assured her that she appeared completely alluring, Flora felt that she looked like a common prostitute.

"Isn't that the point, darling?" he asked as he pulled out a few of her curls to frame her face. "You're meant to draw him in."

Flora glanced at the clock. The midnight hour drew near and the time of her deflowering was almost upon her. As each minute passed by, she grew more and more nervous. "But won't he think me wonton?"

"Not if you're going to him and not some other man."

"He may believe me loose."

"Trust me, darling, once he realizes there's naught but a dainty virgin beneath that powder and lace, he will think nothing other than to make you his."

"Then I suppose I must go now, before I lose my nerve."

Charlie nodded. "Don't fret, Flora. All will be well."

"Do you truly believe so?"

"I believe in you, and that's all that is needed."

***

Flora tiptoed, barefooted, in the dark corridors of the castle, careful to stay in the shadows. She had

Charlie investigate the men's quarters to tell her precisely which room Jasper inhabited, and it was a long way from her own. Each time she heard a distant voice or saw the flicker of light from one of the many candles that lit the hallway, her heart leaped into her throat. But soon she found her mark.

Taking one final brave breath, she pushed open the door and slid into the room, dark save for one single candle Jasper had forgotten to extinguish. She could see a lump in the bed. Jasper lay on his back, deeply asleep and snoring gently.

"Jasper," she whispered, gently touching his arm.

He barely moved.

"Jasper," Flora said a bit louder, jostling him.

The man shot up, his eyes wide and with a dagger in hand. But he withdrew the blade when his gaze settled on Flora, her face hidden by the hood.

"Who's there?" he asked, squinting in the darkness.

Flora pulled back the hood and smiled. "It's me."

"F-Flora?" he gasped, tossing the dagger to the floor and reaching for the candle. "What are ye doin' here?"

"I came to see you."

"It's the wee hour o' the mornin'."

"I know," she replied as he lit another flame.

Jasper studied her, taking in her mass of hair and vivid makeup. His eyes drifted down to the clasp of her cloak. Flora, feeling a spur of courage, unhooked the clasp and let the fabric drop to the floor. Jasper's mouth hung open upon seeing her form in the thin shift. Neither moved for a moment.

58

Each paused and regarded each other, unsure of what to do. But Flora couldn't take the uncertainty and made the first gesture, gently brushing Jasper's cheek with her palm.

Her tender caress broke open the floodgates of desire. Jasper grabbed her by the waist and flung her onto the bed beside him, attacking her mouth with his. Flora's heart beat madly against her breastbone as he nibbled at her lips, his hands roughly groping her chest through the flimsy fabric of her chemise.

She had wondered, the past two years, how it would be between them, and now she knew for certain. At first she thought he might be gentle with her and murmur verses of love in her ear, as the men often did in her romance novels. But no words passed between them and Jasper's probing fingers pinched at her thighs and breasts before briskly pulling her shift over her head and tossing it to the floor.

"Ach, just as pretty as I hoped," he croaked, his eyes grazing her naked body.

Flora's fear eased a bit at his kind compliment. She assumed his coarseness was due to nerves, much as her own meekness was. He did calm his advances a bit as he pulled the coverings off his body. But Flora gasped as she saw he was fully nude, his manhood on display. She averted her eyes, her innards twisting in uncertainly and dread.

"Do no' fret, lass," Jasper soothed, moving to hover above her.

"I'm not afraid." She had tried to sound brave, but her voice quivered.

As Jasper settled between her legs, she held her breath in anticipation. The moment he deflowered her was the moment her life with him could begin. There was no turning back, nor did she want to. She was prepared to give herself to Jasper mind, body, and soul.

Jasper pushed into her with a grunt. The force of his movement jarred her and sent a sharp twinge of pain shooting through her core. She covered her mouth with her palm to keep from crying out in hurt and surprise. The older women of the clan said that it would be uncomfortable and Flora cursed the crones for being right. As Jasper slid in and out, she waited for the waves of pleasure everyone said would come. They had promised pure bliss after the initial penetration. But Flora merely felt squashed.

The act was brief and awkward and Flora wondered why it was nothing as she expected. There were no sweet words, no kissing, and no feeling of joy. Instead, she was brushing her own tangled hair out of her mouth and struggling to breathe under his heavy weight. Her legs lay sprawled on either side of his and his hot breath shot into her ear. Then suddenly, Jasper gave a great shudder and she felt a peculiar sensation *down there*.

He rolled off her body and onto his back, heaving in great gulps of air. Flora drew the sheets back over her form and moved a bit, still feeling rather mussed and sore. She waited for Jasper to hold her in his arms as she thought he would, but he lay there like a big loaf, his breathing slowly steadying.

"Are…are you well?" she questioned, wondering why he had yet to speak.

"Aye, lass," Jasper replied, patting her on the arm. "And you?"

"I'm all right."

"Did ye enjoy it?"

Flora frowned. Certainly he didn't think that she liked being pawed at and roughly handled. But he looked so at peace and happy at that moment that Flora decided to lie. "Very much so."

"Glad to hear it."

"And you?"

"Ach, ye have a fine set o' legs, lass. Verra fine," he mumbled lowly, his eyes closed.

"Are you going to sleep?"

Jasper yawned. "Aye, I thought I might."

Flora bit her lip. She had expecting some kind, gentle words and perhaps some time lying in each other's embrace. His dismissal of her was borderline humiliating. "Oh…I see."

"Ye best be back to your chambers soon, lass. We can no' have ye caught in the halls."

At first, Flora thought that was just what she wanted. But then thought it better to avoid being publically shamed. It would be enough to merely get Conner to support the union and let the rest of the world believe her a maid on her wedding day. She let out an involuntary giggle when she imagined the stunned look on her brother's face when he announced that her marriage to Jasper would then be unavoidable.

"What's so funny?"

"Oh, nothing," Flora sang, beginning to slip from

the bed.

"Are ye off to your own chambers, then?"

She nodded in the dark, snatching her shift from the floor and putting it on quickly. "You're right that I shouldn't be seen."

"Aye, ye took a big risk comin' here," he chastised with a grin. "But I'm glad it's a risk ye decided to take."

Flora smiled in response. His look of happiness heartened her and solidified the idea that she had done the right thing. Certainly their first time had been cumbersome and strange, but they had a whole lifetime to sort through their awkward fumbling and come together as one.

"Goodnight, Jasper," she whispered as she reached the door.

"G'night, lass," he rumbled as he buried himself in his covers.

Flora stepped into the silent corridor and practically ran through the castle in her hurry to get to her bed unnoticed. But as she darted through the hallways and around the sharp corners, she felt a lightness carry her through. Her future was bright and would be full of deep love and new beginnings. Her gamble would pay off threefold and she would soon be married to Jasper.

Chapter Six

"Ye wanted to speak with me?" Conner asked, not looking up from the maps spread upon his desk.

Flora shifted from one foot to the other. The words she needed to say were trapped in her throat, but they needed to come out. They had to, or the events of the night before would be in vain. All she needed to do was tell Conner that she had been bedded and it would all be done and she and Jasper would be hand fasted immediately.

"I…I…" she croaked out. Her palms were sticky with perspiration and she wiped them hastily on the sides of skirt.

"Ye what, Flora?" he sighed, pushing the maps aside and glancing at her.

"I've lain with Jasper and I am no longer a maid!" she blurted out, louder than she intended. Her hands involuntarily slapped over her mouth as she awaited Conner's response.

He clasped his fingers together, his face unreadable. "Is that so?" he whispered after several terse moments.

Flora nodded, unable to speak. She feared she would vomit all over the Persian rug if she opened her mouth.

"And he bedded ye as a husband does his wife?" His voice was still calm, an even tone that didn't give away any hint of emotion.

Flora nodded again.

"And ye know what that means, lass? When a man beds a woman? You are sure o' it?"

Another nod.

"I see." Conner steadily stood from his seat and rolled up his maps, setting each one carefully in the bin beside his chair. Then he brushed past Flora, giving nothing of his thoughts away. He strode briskly through the halls with a very confused Flora at his heels. He seemed so placid, she wasn't truly sure that he understood what she said.

"Conner?" she questioned, jogging to keep pace.

"Aye?"

"Did you…did you hear me correctly?"

"Aye."

Charlotte turned a corner from the opposite direction, baby Alec in her arms. "Oh, hello you two, there—"

"No' now," Conner muttered sharply.

Charlotte turned on her heel as they passed. "Flora, what's going on?"

"I don't know," Flora replied honestly. Nothing was going as planned and now Conner seemed to be going down for a leisurely lunch.

"Good morning," Gwen called out merrily as she came out from one of the rooms. When no one answered her, she joined the little party. "Is everything all right?"

"Conner, what's happened? Tell me now," Charlotte demanded.

"Jasper has bedded Flora and now the lass is no longer a maid," he shot back.

Charlotte gasped and looked at Flora, who felt heat seep up her neck.

"Flora, you didn't!" Gwen cried as all color drained from her face. "Jasper?"

"And where are you going now?" Charlotte asked as they reached the doors to the feasting hall.

"I'm goin' to kill the bastard." Conner kicked open the double doors and marched toward a group of men, drawing his blade as he went.

Flora let out a shrill shriek of alarm. Jasper's blood would spill and it would be her fault.

"Conner, no!" Charlotte yelled.

But he ignored the women and grabbed Jasper by the back of the neck, tossing him to the ground. "Ye bastard! I took ye into my clan when ye had *no one*!" he roared in the now silent hall. "I gave ye food, the clothes on your back, this roof over your bloody head!"

Jasper cringed, curled like a weevil upon the stones. "I-I...Macleod, my laird..."

Conner aimed the point of his sword to the man's throat. "Ye bastard. I'll have your head for this."

"No!" Flora dashed toward them, skittering to the floor and draping her arms over Jasper's quivering form. "You can't!"

"Oh, can't I?" Conner barked out a wry laugh. "I gave him all the care as one o' my own and I gave ye all the freedom—more freedom than ye deserved, apparently. Ye both betrayed me as your laird and I will no' have it."

Flora looked to Charlotte for support, but she merely shook her head. Her gaze hit all the observers in turn, pausing when her eyes met Charlie's. But, for once, his mouth was shut tightly and he looked petrified at such a display. Flora was utterly alone in a room full of people.

"Please Conner, don't kill him," Flora begged, beginning to cry. It humiliated her to beg on her knees his mercy, but she would do whatever it took to save Jasper. "Please!"

Conner nodded toward Big Angus. "Take my wee sister to her chambers and bar the doors."

Flora's blood ran cold. He meant to remove her in order to punish Jasper without her interference. "No, no! Please don't do it. I beg you!"

"Take her now," Conner ordered.

Angus grabbed Flora and flung her over his shoulder like a bag of barley. "Sorry," he whispered as he took her, kicking, from the room.

"And take this sack o' shite to the dungeons," she heard Conner say to someone else.

"Jasper!" Flora screeched, her fists beating Big Angus's back. "Jasper! Jasper!"

Her throat had grown hoarse by the time she was locked in her room. The sound of the lock clicking into place felt like the final nail in the coffin of her heart. Images of Jasper's dead body flashed vividly through her mind. She knew what happened to those who opposed Conner. Before, she had thought that each dead man had deserved his fate and hadn't pitied them as they made their final steps toward Conner's blade. But the mere idea of Conner taking the life of her beloved made her ill and she became violently sick into a chamber pot.

Then she ran to the wall that separated her room from Gwen's and pounded wildly upon it, hoping that Gwen had returned to her chambers and would come to her. But when Flora pressed her cheek to the wall, she heard nothing. She tried opening the door again, but it wouldn't budge, and she knew it was much too sturdy to be forced open. The window wasn't an escape option either, as it faced the sheer cliffs below.

Flora crawled into bed and pulled the blankets over her head, sobbing as she whispered frenzied prayers to the heavens. She called upon God to save her intended, to punish her instead. She begged Him to take back the past day and let her start anew. But as the sun traveled through the sky and began to set, she knew her devotions would be unanswered.

***

The sharp click of the lock jarred Flora from her fitful slumber. Big Angus stood in the doorway looking very meek indeed. She was afraid to speak to him, lest he come to tell her that Jasper had been executed.

"Come with me, please." He held out his hand, his focus on the floor.

"Tell me…does Jasper still live?"

"Aye, though he wishes he did no'."

Flora slipped out of bed and shambled toward

Big Angus, all her strength gone. She held onto his arm as they walked to the receiving room. It was good that the man was so massive; she wouldn't have been able to walk without his strength to carry her through. The thought of what might greet her filled her with unfathomable dread.

When the doors to the receiving room opened, she prepared herself for a gory sight, but the hall was empty, save for Conner upon his throne.

"Flora," he said grimly, his quiet voice echoing against the stone.

She untangled herself from Big Angus's grip and fell to her knees before her brother. "Please…where is Jasper?"

"Ye'll see him soon enough."

Would she? Did Conner plan to send her to the dungeon as well? That would be most cruel, as he knew how afraid of the dark she was. "Please, don't lock me away below."

"Ye are no' goin' to the dungeons," he promised her softly. While his words should have calmed her, she found the tranquil tone of his voice positively terrifying. It was a truly powerful man who needn't raise his voice to strike fear into the hearts of those who opposed him.

"Can I see him? Where is Jasper?"

"Flora, I'm sorry for what ye are about to see."

She felt as though she might faint as she imagined Jasper joining her missing a hand or with another gash across his handsome face, marring him beyond recognition. "Is it so terrible as that?" she sobbed. "Did you have to maim him?"

"He is no' maimed and I will no' kill him."

68

Flora steadied herself as she stood, her knees quaking. "Thank you, Conner."

"Do no' thank me just yet." He looked toward the side door. "Bring him!"

A man entered, dragging Jasper by the arm. He was pushed before the throne and the other man left, leaving the three of them alone. She wanted nothing more than to go to him, but knew it wouldn't help anything. When she did turn to see him, a ghastly sight assaulted her. Deep slashes marked Jasper's back and the blood ran in slowing rivers, staining his plaid. He had been whipped.

"Oh, no." Flora pursed her lips, trying to keep the cries at bay. Jasper did not give so much as a glance in her direction.

"I've ye both here with no witnesses. There is no reason to shame Flora more than ye already have. If she is with bairn, I'll see the child cared for," Conner stated coldly. "Lord knows ye can no' afford another."

"*Another*?" Flora rasped.

"Aye." Conner nodded. "Jasper had kept a lot from us these years. It's time the truth came out."

As if on cue, Big Angus opened the receiving hall doors and a mousy woman in a worn dress marched into the room, her small hands balled into fists. Flora could see flames burn in her gaze, which was fixed upon Jasper. But the woman didn't address him. Instead, she turned to Conner.

"Laird, I'm sorry ye had to deal with my loutish husband," the woman squeaked, her cheeks flushed.

"Husband?" Flora parroted, the room spinning around her. "Jasper?" She waited for him to tell her

69

it wasn't true, to assure her that he had never seen that woman before in his life. But he didn't move.

"Aye," Conner told her. "Flora, meet Blair MacNee, Jasper's wife."

"Wife..." Flora sat back down on the ground, unable to support her own weight. "He's married?"

"Aye, to me!" the woman blustered, glaring at Jasper. "I'm sorry he's done this again, my laird. I can no' get the good-for-nothing to keep his cock in his kilt."

"I-I didn't know he had a wife." Flora buried her face in her hands.

She heard Conner sigh. "Neither did I. It seems he married her a few years ago and only visits to get her with child before runnin' off again. I had no idea."

"Four bairns, laird!" The woman cried. "I've four clingin' to me apron strings and no way to feed them. And this useless oaf had three more by others. I've no use for him. And I'm glad to see him whipped!"

"Shameful," Conner sympathized. "I'll grant ye a divorce, if ye want one. He will no' have any employment in my lands. But I'll see to it that you and the bairns are well cared for."

"Thank ye kindly," the woman said before shifting over toward Flora. "And lass, I'm right sorry he tricked ye so. Ye will no' be the first girl he swayed with a honey tongue, but I hope ye will be the last."

Flora lifted her head, tears streaming down her face. "I'm so sorry. So, so sorry. I didn't know he had a wife. I thought...he said...oh, I'm sorry."

"Do no' fret," the woman soothed, petting Flora gently on the head. "I'm no' harmed by it, for I've seen him for who he is." She then looked back up at Conner. "Might I go, laird? Me sister's with the bairns and my cottage is hours away yet."

Conner nodded. "See Angus as ye leave, he has a bit to help ye through the winter. Come to me if ye need anythin' more."

The woman bobbed a short curtsy and hurried from the room, swearing Jasper under her breath.

"Jasper," Flora bawled. "How *could* you? You have a wife and children! You have a family!"

He didn't answer, but Flora saw his jaw tighten.

"I thought you loved me," she hissed.

"I did," he mumbled, his gaze still on the floor.

"I thought we would be married. Now I could...I could be *with child*!" Flora's shoulders heaved as she sobbed into the hem of her gown.

Conner stepped from her throne and sat beside Flora, placing an arm around her shoulder. "I'm sorry I had to do that."

"I needed to know," Flora sniffed. "I had no idea he was married, I swear."

"I believe ye," Conner assured her. "No one knew. Now I'll leave it up to ye to punish him. Ye may mark him, have him killed, anythin' ye think fair. Tell me what ye wish and I will see it done. "

"I don't know."

"I've already had him flogged and he's lost his farm to his wife, I'll make sure o' that."

Flora slumped against Conner's chest. "I just want him to go. I never want to see him again."

"And ye never will." With a final squeeze,

71

Conner stood, facing Jasper. "Jasper MacNee, I banish ye from my sight and these lands. Ye leave this hall with nothin'. Ye retain no employment, no lands, and no family. Everythin' you own, which I gave ye, will go to your wife for the care of your bairns. Ye are to never step foot in any o' the holdin's o' the MacLeod clan, nor those of our allies. If I catch sight o' ye again, I will send ye to slow death for the crimes ye have committed against my family and yours."

Big Angus, who was posted by the door, stepped forward and lifted Jasper, taking him wordlessly from the room. While Flora despised Jasper now, there was still a part of her, deep down, which held love for him. She had been besotted by the man for two years and had her hopes of a life and family dashed in the course of a day. And he never even said goodbye.

"Come." Conner helped her to stand and half-carried her from the hall. "Let's get ye to bed. Do you care to eat anythin'?"

"No." She didn't feel hungry; she hardly felt anything other than a deep, biting pain that nipped at her soul. "Conner, what have I done?"

"Shhh," he hushed her, leading her toward her chambers. "None o' that now. Ye must rest."

"What…what if I'm with child?"

"We'll deal with it if it comes. Do no' worry over somethin' that may no' come to be."

"I can't have a baby." Flora was being crushed by the reality of her situation. She had given her maidenhead to a terrible man and could be pregnant with his child! While Penelope hadn't gotten herself

72

in the family way, Flora might not be so lucky. The life she envisioned was crashing about around her, burying her in the sheer weight of her own bad decisions.

"Quiet yourself, Flora." Conner opened the door to her chambers, where Gwen sat upon her bed. "All will be better come the morrow."

"Conner, I'm sorry," Flora said, feeling defeated, as she crossed the room to Gwen's open arms. "I never thought this would happen."

Conner shook his head. "Don't. Ye've been punished enough and I will no' make it worse. Gwen, call for me if she worsens tonight, aye?"

"Of course," Gwen answered, helping Flora out of her slippers and between the sheets of her four-poster.

When Conner closed the door behind him, Flora began a fresh wave of sobs. "Gwen, what have I done?"

"Hush, you could never have known." Gwen rubbed her back and brushed the hair from her damp cheeks.

"I was bedded by a married man. He was *married,* Gwen, with children!"

"I know."

Flora choked. "Oh, God…Gwen, does everyone know? I couldn't bear the shame."

"No, don't fret. Conner merely told Charlotte and I when Mrs. MacNee came to the castle. As far as anyone else knows, you two were merely carrying on a flirtation. It's a bad enough offence to warrant Jasper's banishment, but not so terrible as to ruin your reputation."

"I suppose I should feel pleased, but I just can't."

Gwen said nothing. She merely kicked off her own shoes and slid into bed with Flora as she had often done as a little girl. She intertwined their fingers and offered Flora the gift of silent companionship and blameless soothing. Flora briefly wondered what she had done to deserve such a kind soul.

"Gwen...what do I do now?"

Her younger sister paused thoughtfully before replying. "You grieve and then you carry on as you did before. You live your life and meet a nice man and have a lovely family and never speak of these things again. I know things look horrid right now, but this will pass."

"I'm no longer a maid, Gwen," Flora admitted, felling a deep shame at her verbal pronouncement. "I laid with Jasper as a wife does her husband...but he was already someone else's husband!"

"It's not the end of the world. Men dally around with women for far less noble reasons than love. You loved him dearly and that doesn't make you wrong. It doesn't make you a terrible person."

"But it is. What respectable man would want me? I've destroyed my future because I thought some man loved me."

"Don't speak of yourself as if you are ruined, Flora," Gwen ordered fiercely, her grip tightening. "You're a beautiful, intelligent, caring lady who got carried away and made *one* bad decision. Anyone who judges you based on one night isn't worth knowing."

"Oh, Gwen, I wish everyone thought like you.

The world would be a much more pleasant place to live."

"And no one will gossip about you, either," she declared. "If they do, I'll…I'll box them round the ears."

Flora giggled at that, the sound tasting odd in her mouth, but it was still a welcomed reprieve from crying. "I'd like to see that, truly I would."

"If it would help, I'll go find an unsuspecting victim and give them a good thrashing."

"As much as that would amuse me, there's been enough dramatics for one day."

Gwen nodded pulled the blanket over Flora's shoulders. "Would you like to speak of it?"

"I don't know if I should."

"Just because he was never yours doesn't mean you can not grieve for him. Your feelings are valid and true, even if you're the only one who understands them. Or we can lay in silence and speak of him no more."

Flora didn't answer her. She merely lay in the dark, watching the flickering light of slowly melting candle at her bedside. She imagined the wax as her feelings, gradually melting away to nothing, as did her dreams.

Chapter Seven

"Darling Flora, might I come in?" Charlie poked his head in the half opened door.

Flora lifted her head off her pillow and grunted, bidding him entrance. She had avoided Charlie for two straight days. As a matter of fact, she had avoided everyone for two days, save Gwen, who spent many hours sitting beside the window, practicing her needlepoint. But Flora supposed she had to face the rest of the world at some point and might as well start with Charlie.

"Is she…is she well?" Charlie asked Gwen quietly as he tiptoed in.

"I'm sad, not dead," Flora muttered as she pulled herself upright and tucked her knees to her chin.

Charlie teetered on his heels, his eyes flitting about the room. She was about to tell him to speak or leave when he opened his mouth. "Flora…I've been beating myself up over what happened and I wanted to come and apologize for…helping you…I just wanted…oh, Flora, do forgive me." He knelt down beside the bed.

"Charlie, there's nothing to forgive," she told him earnestly. "Everything was my idea, you only assisted me in what I wanted to do. You're quite innocent in this manner."

"Still, I feel so horribly. What will you do now?"

Flora sighed. "I'm not quite sure. I suppose I'll have to stay here until…"

"Until what?" Charlie asked.

"Until she knows if she is with child," Gwen answered calmly, her eyes still upon the delicate roses she had been stitching.

"Well then." Charlie cleared his throat. "Flora, I've been thinking…why not come away from Scotland for a spell? You've been wanting to go back to England for so long and a change of pace might do you well."

"Wouldn't that just be running from my problems?"

"Hardly. It would be a lovely diversion and a chance to reflect," he replied smartly.

"As much as I would love to escape to London, I don't think Conner would dare let me out of his sight."

Charlie's face split into a grin that showed off his brilliantly white teeth. "Well, don't fret, darling, because old Charles has sorted everything."

"What do you mean?"

"I mean that I've already spoken to the lovely Charlotte MacLeod about how terribly you're doing and how her parents have been *so* upset at not being able to their grandson more often," he explained, practically bouncing in his excitement. "She sees the merit in a trip to London, and as your brother has stopped counting sheep, or whatever it is he does here, it's a perfect time to go on a holiday."

Flora felt her lips curl upward. The idea of fleeing Scotland for the bustle of the city pleased her. "Truly?"

"Truly." Charlie nodded.

"And when will we leave?"

"As soon as you get your lovely self packed and ready to take the carriage to the train!" He stood and strode over to his wardrobe. "Yes, yes, we'll just shove all this in a crate and ship to London. But we must hurry, as I've just gotten word that there's a train leaving in a few hours."

Flora giggled and slid out of bed, pulling a dressing gown over her shift. "Would I have time to bathe?"

"Certainly," Charlie assured her, ringing the servant's bell. "You go get pretty and I'll have things sorted for our departure."

Gwen put down her needlework and followed Flora into the bathroom. "I'll miss you when you leave."

"Then come with us," Flora suggested as she turned on the water, filling the tub. "Since you left finishing school, you've hardly been to London at all."

Gwen shrugged and sat on the edge of the porcelain as Flora undressed and lowered herself into the water. "I don't much care for London."

"You can't just sit in the castle and sew. Come with me."

"I have my whole life for adventuring, Flora. There's an entire world I could see anytime I wish.

But once I marry and have a family of my own, I will leave this castle and only return as a guest, as our sisters do. I'll enjoy the quiet of the hills and the routine of the castle for now and go on grand travels one day."

"Gwendolyn, for someone so young, you are quite wise."

"I'm not that young." Gwen pouted dramatically, crossing her arms over her chest. But with her mass of golden curls and dimpled cheeks, she looked very much like a little china doll. While she acted far older than her years, she still appeared much more youthful than most eighteen-year-olds.

"Fine, you win. You're an elderly spinster."

Gwen smiled and splashed Flora before leaping from her perch and running from the room before Flora could retaliate. As much as Flora enjoyed Gwen's light company, she was thankful for her final few moments alone with her thoughts before boisterous Charlie bore her to the MacLeod home in London. She decided her best course of action was to accept every invitation, attend every gathering, and generally fill her day completely until she was too tired to think of anything but sleep.

"Come now, Flora," Charlie called from the other side of the closed door. "I can't be seen on the train with a big prune."

Flora laughed and pulled herself reluctantly from the comforting waters. While the bath did little to wash away all that had happened, it was a start.

***

"Will you be all right on your own for a few days while we settle things here?" Charlotte asked, holding tight to Flora's arm.

"I'll have Charlie with me on the way," Flora assured her. "He won't let me come to any harm."

"Aye, he will no'." Conner eyed up Charlie, who returned his dagger-filled look with a jolly raise of his ginger brows. "Ach, enough o' that nonsense."

"I will keep her safe from all harm, my liege." Charlie bobbed a clumsy bow.

Conner grunted and turned to Flora. "Ye will be well, aye? I can always send Charlotte with ye now. Or at least some servants?"

"Don't. I'll be fine. You need all the hands you can spare to clean up after the wedding." Flora tried to look as if she was sound, but she knew from the mirror on her dressing table that her blotchy face and puffed eyes told the true story.

He passed her a sealed envelope. "Give this to the housekeeper. She's to know to prepare for my arrival and that ye are the lady o' the manor until then."

"And I suppose you've told her to keep a tight rein on me as well?" Flora grimaced. The housekeeper, Mrs. Neely, believed the woman's place was securely in the home at all times.

"I've told her no such thing." Conner pulled her into a tight embrace. "Ye've been punished enough these past days. I will no' cage a wounded bird."

Flora bit her lip against the tears that threatened to spill. "Oh, Conner I'm—"

"If ye apologize one more time, I'll send ye to a nunnery," he promised, kissing her gruffly on the

Kelsey McKnight

side of the head, then pushing her toward the carriage. "Go, and for the love of all that's holy, do no' listen to anythin' Charlie tells ye."

***

"I *still* can't believe he thinks me a bad influence." Charlie sniffed as their carriage rolled over the dark, uneven London roads. A late night fog had thickened the air, making their journey more jostling than usual. "*Me*, of all people! Honestly, I'm shocked and appalled."

"You stuck your hand up someone's kilt on the morning of Penelope's wedding after too many glasses of wine and shrieked that you found the Holy Grail."

"If you had felt what *I* had, you'd say the same."

Flora let out a burst of giggles, both amused and horrified at his words. "You're terrible."

Charlie leaned forward, eager to tell her more. "Really, Flora, it was massive. It was as if it belonged to a—"

"*Horse!*" their driver yelled and the sound of sharp whinny cut through the air.

The carriage screeched to a halt and Flora fell from her seat and into Charlie's arms. "What on earth was that racket?"

Charlie helped her up before hopping to the street. "Is everything all right?"

Flora popped her head out the door and could see a lone horse with a man atop. "What's happened?"

"Sorry, miss," the driver said from behind one of their horses. "That rotten rider galloped before the

81

carriage and I think this old gal threw a shoe."

"What does that mean?" Charlie asked, checking his pocket watch in the dim light.

"It means that it's unsafe for the horse to go any farther without being seen to," Flora explained.

"So that man is keeping us out until morning?" Charlie pointed to the rider, who leaped from his perch and awkwardly walked over to them, stumbling over the cobblestones.

"I'm so sorry, the horse just…got away from me," the figure said.

When he stepped closer to a streetlight and removed his hat, Flora could see clearly who it was. "Andrew Philips?"

He squinted in response. "Flora MacLeod?"

"Charles, Duke of Fenton," Charlie quipped, tucking his timepiece back into his breast pocket. "Now that we've gotten that nonsense out of the way, what will we do now? It's not as if we can just abandon our luggage. I have a cape in there I *need* for the opera, Flora. The opera!"

"Take my horse," Andrew blurted out.

Flora shook her head. "We couldn't do that and leave you stranded."

"I wouldn't be," Andrew assured her. "That's my townhome, just there. I'll take your injured horse to be looked at by my man and you can finish your travels."

"Are you certain it wouldn't put you out?" Flora glanced at the building he had gestured to, and it was only a very short stroll down the road. But she still hated to inconvenience anyone.

"Flora, the man said we could borrow his horse,

82

and borrow it we shall." Charlie thumped Andrew upon the back. "Jolly good, Andrew. Or *Andy*! Might I call you Andy?"

"I-I suppose so..." Andrew replied, giving the reins to the carriage driver to make the exchange.

Charlie clapped his hands together. "Splendid. Well, *Andy,* where were you off to in such a bluster?"

"I had word that a certain novel I've had my eye on at the national library had just been made available for service." He buried about in his satchel to product a brown leather bound book with worn edges. "It spans the laws of the early Ottoman empire. You know, they had—"

"Magnificent," Charlie declared, cutting off Andrew. "Now that we have everything sorted, do come for tea tomorrow. Flora and I should be quite recovered by then, and I could return your horse."

"Oh, yes, certainly," Flora agreed. "We must repay your kindness somehow."

Andrew shuffled his feet a bit. "Hardly a kindness, as my flighty horse is what caused this entire ordeal."

"Still, you didn't have to lend us your horse." Flora thought his shyness was rather amusing, especially as it was no longer accompanied with the initial stuttering he had when they first met.

"I couldn't leave you out in the night," Andrew said softly, tucking his book back into his bag. "I would never forgive myself if any harm came to your person because of something I did."

"I'll be quite all right," she promised. "But it's sweet of you to worry so."

"Yes, it's all rather adorable." Charlie yawned. "But now might we go? The horses are settled and it's high time I get into bed with a bottle of brandy."

"We'll see you tomorrow for tea?" Flora asked finally as she began her assent into the carriage.

"I wouldn't miss it," Andrew replied, taking the lead of the injured horse.

"I wouldn't miss it," Charlie crooned in a dramatic falsetto as they began their drive toward the MacLeod home.

"Do shut up!" spat Flora, turning to look out the window. Muggy yellow clouds of fog hung beneath each light post.

"Isn't he the fellow who dragged your inebriated self up to your chambers the night of Penelope's wedding?"

Flora's glare shot toward Charlie. "I told you we were never to speak of that night again."

"Yes, you told me, but I rarely listen. Honestly, Flora, you should know this by now." Charlie shifted in his seat a bit. "I'm rather shocked he could carry you, as small as he is. Are you sure it wasn't the other way around?"

"Stop it, Charlie. You're acting like he's a frail child. I can tell you that he delivered me safely up an entire flight of stairs."

"I think he's quite…what's the word?" He tapped his chin thoughtfully. "I wouldn't call him dashing, nor fierce. Perhaps…endearing? Yes, that's the world. *Endearing.*"

"Endearing is such a pitiful term."

"Fitting for a pitiful man."

Flora jarred. It seemed a rather harsh statement.

84

"You think him pitiful?"

Charlie rolled his eyes. "He dashed out in the middle of the night for a book on Mongols."

"The Ottoman empire."

"Pish-posh. Either way, he's just a soft little chap who reminds me of a lost puppy. The way he gushes over you is shameful."

"He doesn't gush over me, that's ridiculous."

"Ridiculously true."

Flora turned away from him again and her thoughts drifted toward gentle Andrew Philips, who was never anything but perfectly polite, no matter the circumstances. And the circumstances they often met in were anything but orthodox. Once they were thrust together when Flora was lying on the floor unable to move and now they practically ran him over in the middle of the night. At least tea would be nothing more than a completely appropriate meeting.

***

"Flora, should we spike the tea?" Charlie asked, a flask poised over the blue china teapot. He wriggled his ginger brows.

She snatched it from his grasp and scowled. "Certainly not. We're having a perfectly respectable *tea*, not a grand bash."

"Might as well." He flopped onto the couch and dropped a small teacake into his mouth. "Talking with that Philips fellow bores me to tears."

"Be nice. You're the one who invited him to tea, so the least you could do is be polite."

85

"Mister Andrew Philips," a butler announced, shepherding a timid looking Andrew through the doors.

"Andy, old boy!" Charlie sat up and strode over to Andrew, taking him by the hand and showing him to an armchair. "Glad you could come."

"Good afternoon, Andrew," Flora greeted as she poured him a cup of tea.

"Thank you both for inviting me. I still feel terribly about last night," Andrew admitted, adjusting his jacket. "I didn't know you would both be back in London so soon after the wedding."

Charlie plopped back down on the couch beside Flora, making her cushion bounce. "Well, we thought we'd catch the last of the fall shows and make all of our Christmas purchases early."

"So you won't be staying long?" Andrew asked, drinking his tea black.

Flora picked up her own cup and took a sip before puckering. The leaves must have been bitter, or had steeped too long. She dropped two more sugar cubes into the brew, which made it much more bearable. Charlie, she could see, had no issues with his beverage, as he rapidly drained two cups.

"Might I ask where these leaves hail from?" Andrew peered at the dregs at the bottom of the china. "I don't believe I've ever had this before. It's an...unusual blend."

Charlie's eyes bulged as he clamped his lips shut.

Flora knitted her brow, instantly suspicious. "What is it?"

"It's a *special* blend," Charlie croaked between

strangled chuckles. "One of my own making."

She opened up the pot and looked inside, seeing nothing out of the ordinary. Nonetheless, Flora put down her cup and turned on Charlie. "What did you do?"

"I thought I'd just spice things up a bit." Charlie pulled a small flask from his pocket and gave it a good-natured peck.

Flora glanced at the container she had taken earlier, which still sat on the side table. "Where did that come from?"

"A gentleman always keeps an emergency flask," he declared, taking a little nip. "Isn't that right, Andy?"

"Quite," Andrew responded evenly, pushing away his cup.

"Pardon me," the butler interrupted. "A Matthew Elmsly has come to call. Are you at home?"

"Hark!" Charlie sprang from his seat and straightened his jacket. "My Romeo doth approach."

Flora hung her head, only looking back up when she heard the sitting room doors slam shut. "Andrew, I'm terrible sorry for Charlie's behavior. I promise we're not all total loons. I'm ever so embarrassed."

"Please, don't think of it. He's much more lively than anyone at university. It's rather a nice diversion."

"He's lively to a fault," she muttered. "I am terribly sorry for the tea. I would have never served it to you, had I known."

"It's quite all right. I don't usually take tea

anyway outside of the morning."

"No tea?" Flora thought that particularly odd, as she'd never met an Englishman who didn't down the stuff by the pot.

He shook his head, glancing about the room. Flora then became acutely aware that he hadn't made eye contact with her once since entering the sitting room. She shifted uncomfortably in her seat, mindful of the silence that surrounded them and the way Andrew's foot tapped upon the floor, as if he was counting the passing seconds.

The awkward stillness made Flora wonder why Andrew was suddenly acting so strange with her. The night of Penelope's wedding, when he helped her up to her chambers, she vaguely remembered his openness and the way he assisted her without judgment and perhaps even shared a laugh with her. Even the morning after, he had said goodbye pleasantly, without the stuttering or the bleak silence that now assaulted them. She had to do something to break the quiet.

"Andrew—"

"Flora—"

"Oh, I'm sorry, you first," she said.

He held up his hands. "No, please, as you were saying?"

"I-I was just going to inquire as to how your studies are progressing," she replied lamely. She could kick herself for her inability to spark a true conversation and regressing to such idle chat.

"Very well, thank you," he answered, his gaze still traveling from his shoes, to the fireplace, and to the window beyond Flora's head. "I have my final exams just before the Christmas holidays."

She very much wished he would just look at *her* instead of everything else possible. "And then what are your plans?"

"I can practice law anywhere, really, but I believe I will be staying in London to take over my uncle's practice."

"You must be pleased. Higher education is a very time consuming but worthwhile pursuit."

"Exceedingly." Andrew pursed his lips and Flora saw him redden about the ears. Then be opened his mouth. "Flora...would you care to attend the opera with me?"

She paused, almost stunned at his request. "I-I—"

"About damned time," Charlie declared, striding into the room followed by a disheveled looking Matthew.

"Pardon?" Andrew questioned, his voice no longer timid but full of that masculine body Flora found oddly appealing.

"I said that it's about time you got around to asking Flora on an evening about the town." Charlie plucked his first flack off the side table and tossed it to Matthew. "And what opera shall you be attending?"

Andrew cleared his throat, obviously uncomfortable being stared at by three people. "I recently acquired tickets for tomorrow night to see *La Fanciulla di Vanezia*."

"Is that the new Italian one about the prostitutes?" Matthew piped in, twirling his mustache as always.

"Well…I wouldn't say that exactly…" Andrew mumbled, his cheeks radiating red. Flora pitied him.

"I've read that it's a marvelous show," she injected smoothly, smiling warmly at Andrew. In truth, she knew nothing of the opera, or any other for that matter.

"And will you be joining Andy at the opera, my darling Flora?" Charlie questioned, patting an uncomfortable-looking Andrew upon the shoulder.

"Yes, I will."

Andrew's face split into a straight-toothed grin, which she thought made him look boyishly handsome in a way she found charming. The lock of auburn hair that fell loosely over his forehead only highlighted it. His brown eyes flitted to her appreciatively and Flora had to look away, lest she adopt her own blush at his enthusiasm.

Andrew stood then, keeping the deep voice he seemed to only use with other men. "Charles, thank you for the invitation to tea. Flora, where should I collect you tomorrow evening?"

"Right to it, this one," Charlie whispered loudly to Matthew.

"The MacLeod townhome is quite close to the Elmsly one." She pointed to a small silver tray where her calling cards sat. "Charlie, please pass Andrew my card."

Charlie picked two, handing both over. "Just in case you lose one, old chap."

"Thank you," Andrew said amiably. Flora noted that he had no problem looking directly at Charlie and Matthew, but he wouldn't look at her without reason. "Good day."

Flora watched him leave, feeling very strange about the entire encounter. Charlie squinted at the door and frowned while Matthew yawned and helped himself to the alcoholic tea that still sat largely untouched before them.

"Flora," Charlie began, taking a teacake. "What do you believe is on young Andy's mind?"

"What do you mean?"

"I mean to say that he's a rather nervous man who I believe couldn't give one fig about the opera." Charlie leaned in closer. "But I do think he's rather interested in *you*."

Flora balked, her cheeks flaming. "Oh, no, he's just being polite."

Charlie raised a brow before turning to his companion. "Matthew, what do you think of all this?"

Matthew looked up from his cup. "If you will both pardon my forwardness on the matter, I believe he has taken an interest in Miss MacLeod."

She stood, motioning for Charlie to follow. "May I speak with you a moment in the hall?"

Charlie shoved the rest of his cake into his mouth and followed her into the deserted corridor. "You do know that Matthew won't betray your secrets. After all, he and I share more than a few."

"I could care less what happens in your bedchambers at present. I think we need to speak about Andrew Philips."

"What about him?"

"Are you convinced he's fond of me?"

"Exceedingly so. Take his manner of speech. Before Matthew and I, he's reserved but he's still capable to giving a commanding presence. However, with you, he's all thumbs and nerves and flitting about like a poor little kitten who's lost his way."

"You know, I've noticed a bit of the same." Flora felt oddly validated that she hadn't just imagined his tameness around her.

"Well, what are you going to do then?"

"What do you mean?"

He rolled his eyes. "Must I spell everything out?"

"Apparently."

"He's taken a shine to you. I think he might be under the impression that you could make a fine love interest."

Flora shook her head madly. "Goodness, no!"

"No need to be so brash about it." Charlie laughed. "He's rather handsome—clear skin, broad of shoulder, and a full head of hair that rivals only my own in terms of body and favorable hue."

"It's not his looks that worry me."

The grin vanished from Charlie's round face. "What is it?"

Flora looked around, making sure they were very alone. "It's just…everything that's happened is just so fresh."

"Well, the best way to get over a man is to get under a new one…or behind one, whatever your preference is in the matter."

Flora grimaced. "That's not really what I had in mind. I mean to say that I'm not even sure…when Jasper and I…he…" Flora moaned, unable to find the words she needed to say.

"You fear you could be with child," he stated gently.

Flora nodded.

He threw an arm around her shoulders and gave her arm a little squeeze. "There's no use worrying over something that may never come to be. I know you're frightened, but there's no need to punish yourself more than you already have."

"Perhaps I should tell him I can't come to the opera?"

"Why would you do a silly thing like that?"

"I wouldn't want to lead him on, if things could never…if I could not…" Flora slumped against him. "Oh, what on earth am I to do?"

"Well, I'll tell you what you are to do. You're going to wear a lovely gown, your best jewels, and go to the opera with Andy and be your utterly charming self. If I recall, you were quite the society darling last time you took over London."

A smile coaxed itself from Flora's lips.

"There it is! Come out of this darkness and have a nip of brandy with Matthew and I. No more talk of that stupid Scottish oaf, nor your worries."

"Easier said than done," muttered Flora. But she followed Charlie back into the drawing room anyway, eager to forget her troubles.

Chapter Eight

"Am I making a mistake in going?" Flora asked Charlie as a maid laced up her corset.

"Not at all," he replied, looking her over before addressing the maid. He had brought the girl from his own kitchens to the MacLeod's household in lieu of Flora being without any servants. "Tighter, girl. If Flora can breathe, then it's no good."

Flora held her breath as she was cinched even tauter, pressing the stays into her ribs. "Goodness, I can't breathe now."

"That's the point." He dug a bit more through her box of jewels and picked up an opal necklace and matching earrings. "Think of how glorious your bust will look in your canary silks."

"This is an awful lot of trouble to go through for just Andrew Philips." Flora shifted a bit, trying to acclimate her lungs to the shallow breaths she was being forced to take.

"You need some good fun and what safer way to test the waters than with innocent, safe, little Andy?"

"I suppose you're right," Flora admitted as the borrowed maid began helping her into her deep yellow gown.

Charlie passed her the fiery opals and watched as she put them on. "You know, I've been doing a bit of research lately—"

"If you're about to tell me about some midnight rendezvous, please don't."

"Oh, it's nothing to with *my* midnight rendezvous and everything to do with *your* potential ones."

Flora's eyes flitted to the maid, who didn't look very surprised by their conversation. "What do you mean?"

"I went down to the club today and asked around about Andy. We don't really know him after all."

"Oh? And what did you find out?" Flora powdered her nose gently as the maid started to rapidly twist her hair atop her head. She tried to take a deep breath, but her chest felt very constricted. It meant for a night of very shallow breathing.

"A whole lot of nothing interesting," he moaned, flopping into an armchair. "He's so terribly...*average*. He has a sizeable fortune, but doesn't gamble nor overspend. He's three and twenty years of age, yet has never taken a mistress so far as anyone knows. He's the member of several societies in London, but always follows the rules."

"Is that so bad? I do believe I could do with some average."

"Well, it's rather boring. You see, he was born into moneyed parents, nothing as grand as you or I, but comfortable. They own some land and gave him a good education. He has a younger brother in the Queen's army in India, but hasn't served, himself. He stands to take over his uncle's practice in the next year or two, which does rather well."

"All good things."

Charlie took out his flask from his breast pocket. "Too good."

A knock on the door jarred them both and Flora called out, "Enter!"

The housekeeper Mrs. Neely entered. "Mister Philips is here to collect ye, Miss."

"Thank you, Mrs. Neely." Flora stood and crossed the room to her full-length mirror. "Please ready my sable furs."

"Will this lass be goin' with ye?" Mrs. Neely gestured to the borrowed maid.

Flora fluffed out her skirts as she studied herself, noting that Charlie had been correct in his assumption of her bosom. "No, I will be attending the opera without a chaperone this evening."

Mrs. Neely pursed her lips, looking rather unhappy about Flora leaving with a strange man, but apparently knew better than to press the matter. She disappeared out of the room.

"Old bat looks like she's swallowed a lemon," Charlie muttered.

"Do I look all right?" Flora asked, adjusting the large opal at her throat.

"A vision, darling. Andy won't be able to keep his hands off you."

Flora watched as her reflection pinked and she brought her gloved hand to her chest, covering her cleavage. "I don't know if I want that."

"Don't worry, it's merely a turn of phrase. I doubt Andy would have the strength to look at you, let along lay a finger on you. Poor chap might burst into flames at the first thought."

Flora giggled a bit and began toward the door. "Be nice, Charles."

"I'm always nice."

Once Flora stepped to the top of the stairs, she could see Andrew waiting below, wearing a black overcoat and clutching a top hat in his fist. She could see he had even fixed his hair so it sat in a perfect deep auburn wave. His brown eyes widened when he saw Flora and he didn't look away until she had made it to the landing below.

"G-good evening, Miss MacLeod," Andrew stammered, his face white.

"Good evening." She allowed Mrs. Neely to help her into fur stole. "I do hope I haven't kept you waiting long?"

"No, not at all," Andrew assured her, putting his hat back on. "Please, my carriage is waiting outside."

"Have fun, you two," Charlie cooed from the steps.

Andrew nodded up at him and allowed Flora to step first into the dark night. She saw he had a rather nice carriage with an agreeably matched pair of dappled greys. He held out his hand and helped her up into the seat. Once he had taken his place across from her, they began their journey to the opera house in awkward silence.

"So…" Flora wracked her brain for something

say, but came up empty. The quiet was rather unsettling. Not to say she was afraid of Andrew, but she wished she knew how to interact with him.

"Miss MacLeod, you look lovely this evening."

Flora allowed herself to relax, as much as she could despite her corset. "Thank you very much. And, please, I've told you before that such formalities are not needed. Call me Flora."

"Well…Flora," he said quietly as he looked out the small window to his left. "Tell me, do you like the opera?"

"Truth be told, I've never been."

"Then I hope you enjoy yourself this evening. The show should be quite good."

"Do you go very often?"

"To the opera? No I can't say that I do."

Flora tried taking a deep breath, but it was stifled in her chest. Feeling constricted, she shimmied a bit in her bodice, trying to loosen the tightness that crushed her. But she couldn't find a position in which to breathe more comfortably.

"Are you cold?" Andrew asked her gently, his face a mask of concern.

She waved a hand and tried to smile. "Oh, I'm fine."

By the time they reached the opera house, Flora found it exceedingly painful to gasp more than the most meager of pants of air. Damning the corsets and those who made them to hell, Flora whipped out her fan and began flapping it wildly, trying to inhale the cool breeze as they exited the carriage and joined the throngs of society.

She saw several familiar faces, and even noticed

Andrew tipping his hat at a few, but couldn't bring herself to speak to any of them. The precious air it would take seemed too much. Instead, she gripped Andrew's arm for dear life and allowed him to escort her through the crowds and into their private box.

"Lovely seats," she whispered as she lowered herself into her chair and attempted to get comfortable. But it was easier said than done.

"Are you sure you're quite well?" Andrew leaned in toward her as the opera house dimmed and the orchestra tuned their instruments.

A butler passed her a glass of something, but she feared she couldn't even take a sip, for there was no room in her stomach. "Very!" Flora quipped, fluttering her fan and attempting a smile. "I'm just very excited."

Andrew grinned a bit, showing off a pair of perfectly cut dimples. Flora didn't recall seeing them before and they made his clean features look a bit less polished, more rugged, although not in a terrible way. It gave her something to focus on other than the squeezing pressure assaulting her torso. So she studied his smooth locks of chestnut hair and the way he spun the signet upon his finger. Flora also noted that his eyes glanced her way at each crescendo, as if waiting for her to respond.

But by the time the opera was midway through, Flora could take the strain of her stays no longer. "Andrew," she hissed at the singer slowed to a low tune. "Is there no intermission?'

"I don't believe so," he replied in a hush. "Would you care for a fresh drink?"

Flora bit her lip. "No, no, I'm fine."

Andrew turned in his seat, looking at her in a very serious manner. "Flora, please tell me what is bothering you. Lying does you no good."

She huffed in exasperation, ashamed for what she was about to say aloud. "It's my…my *corset*."

"Your…" Andrew's eyes narrowed for a moment, then widened. "Oh…*oh*!"

"I must go to the powder room and have one of the maids remedy the situation." She rose from her seat, hurrying to run from the mortifying position she found herself in. All she wanted was to watch a nice opera with a nice man and there she was, feeling as if she would faint. "Do excuse me."

"Wait, I'll escort you." Andrew followed her from the box and down the stairs.

"Please, go enjoy the show," Flora pleaded outside the ladies dressing room. "I won't be but a moment."

"I'll wait here," he assured her.

Flora rushed into the power room, excited for someone to finally loosen her stays. But the room was empty and no one came to assist when she called out. She felt the hot tears of embarrassment prick her eyelids. It was only her first night out trying to forget, and she was on the verge of collapse because Charlie ordered her blasted corset be strung too tight.

Andrew was still smiling when Flora practically dragged herself from the dressing room. She felt ridiculously lightheaded and wanted nothing more than to cut the laces of her gown then and there.

"Everything well?" Andrew questioned, noting

her flushed face.

"Not quite."

"What happened?"

"There wasn't anyone there," she explained and she struggled to catch her breath.

Andrew went to her side and placed a firm arm around her waist. "Should we leave? I'll call for the carriage."

The room began to spin and Flora leaned into him. "I need you...I need you to help me."

His eyes were wide in alarm. "Tell me, what can I do?"

"Loosen my corset," she rasped. "I can't do it on my own and there's no one else."

"Oh...all right," he mumbled, his white face glowing a vibrant shade of red.

Flora pulled him into the ladies' dressing room and turned her back to him. "Hurry, please."

She felt his shaking fingers make quick work of the buttons along her back then felt a rush of breath enter her lungs as her stays were released. She stood there a moment, swallowing in air and relishing the feeling of having full mobility of her torso.

"Is that...was that...are you...well?"

Flora smiled in relief then felt a vivid splash of awareness that she had instructed a perfect stranger to practically undress her. So much for getting back on her social feet. "Andrew, would you be so kind as to fasten my gown, please? Only loosely, this time."

"Certainly."

Once she was fastened into her dress, with more room to breathe, she slowly turned to face him.

"I'm so terribly sorry about that. I'm so very embarrassed."

"Don't be," he told her, his eyes skittering about the room. "Should we retire for the evening or go back to our seats?"

Flora's mind went to her loosened stays, but she had to admit that she felt rather bruised about the middle. "Would you be cross if we were to leave?"

"Hardly," he replied, his warm gaze sincere. "I'll call for my carriage and return you home at once."

"Lovely," Flora replied stiffly. As soon as he had left the room, a sick burst of laughter burst from her lips. It was a mixture of incredulous tears of shame and hilarious giggles that tore her sides. The sheer insanity of the moments before had confused her emotions beyond all sense. She struggled to shove the conflicting sensations back inside, but found it almost impossible. Only when she heard a light knock on the door did she stop.

Flora dabbed at her eyes and smoothed her hair before turning the knob.

"I've fetched our coats." Andrew helped her into her stole before donning his own jacket and hat. "Are you sure you're all right?"

"I am many things at present, but I suppose 'all right' is one of them." Flora ruffled her furs a bit, hoping to hide some of the blush in her cheeks.

Andrew helped her up the steps to the carriage and gave her what she supposed was meant to be a reassuring smile. "Are you sure you aren't in need of a doctor?"

"Goodness, no." She trained her eyes out the carriage window. "I can't begin to tell you how sorry I am for making you miss the opera."

"Please, don't think of it. There will be many more operas."

"It just seems that, as of late, you've had to assist me in far too many embarrassing situations."

"Only two," he pointed out in a lighthearted manner that coaxed a smile from Flora's lips.

"And that is two too many, in my opinion."

"Don't worry, you're perfectly charming when you're exceedingly inebriated or suffering from lack of oxygen."

"You're perfectly horrid."

"No, I'm perfectly right." He grinned in such a way that a single dimple was seen, cut deep into his cheek. Even in the scant light from the passing lampposts, it was clear he thought the entire exchange was hilarious. As his shoulders shook with silent laughter, a single lock of dark auburn hair fell from it's perfectly pressed coif.

Flora felt a quick flash of something strange hit her belly as she fought the urge to reach out and tuck it back into place. It was the same feeling she got when Jasper had gently touched her in the halls of the MacLeod keep, but still different. It was almost as if she thought she should feel ashamed for any feelings of attraction toward Andrew, no matter how fleeting.

When the carriage stopped before the townhome, she was almost sad that their journey had come to an end. In silence, he assisted her to the street and escorted her to the front door. They paused at the top of the stairs on the wide stone landing, each looking down at the ground, the door, the carriage, anything but each other.

"Flora, I did have a nice time with you tonight, all dressing issues aside."

"Ha-ha," she retorted dryly, but with a slight smile. His cheek was infectious.

"Would you like to go out again one evening? Or day, if you'd rather?"

Her eyes turned up toward him, completely astonished that he would ever want to speak with her again, let alone take her out in public. "If you would be agreeable, yes. Yes, I would."

"Wonderful. Then I shall call upon you soon?"

"I'd like that," she told him honestly.

Andrew leaned forward, quiet suddenly, and brushed his lip against the apple of her cheek before pulling away. "Have a good night, Flora."

Too stunned by his action to say much else, she managed, "Have a good night, Andrew."

She left then, quick to let herself into the dim parlor. Leaning against the closed door, she listened to the far-off sound of Andrew's carriage rolling away over the cobblestones before letting out a deep breath she didn't know was trapped within her chest. He didn't tease, make promises, nor push beyond her limits. He wanted to see her again, finding her charming through her faults.

And the next morning, when Flora awoke, there was a tall vase of pink azaleas upon her nightstand. A small card was tucked between lush, green leaves and when she opened it, in simple script it read:

Although you were the one to lose your breath, you always take mine away.

Chapter Nine

"Such sweet adoration! Poor lamb." Charlie tossed the card that accompanied Flora's flowers to the ground.

"He's not a *poor lamb*," Flora shot hotly, scooping the card from the floor and tucking it into her bodice for safekeeping. "I was only showing you because I thought you'd like to know."

"Oh, I did want to know. I've been dying to hear how your night on the town with a wet towel went."

"That's a rather cruel thing to say." She crossed her arm and turned her nose upward. "I suppose I won't tell you a thing then if you'll be so negative about Andrew."

Charlie gasped and threw himself to the ground at her feet, his hands clasped before him. "Don't do that to me, Flora! Have a heart! I've been dying to know how little Andy handled my favorite highland lass."

Flora smirked despite herself. "Fine, I'll tell you. But no more poking fun at Andrew. He was very kind to me last evening and I find myself indebted to his kindness."

He rose and deposited himself on his couch as Flora sat gracefully in the armchair closest to the fire. "Tell me, what happened?"

"We got the opera house and I noticed that my corset was too tight. It felt as if it was stopping me from taking real breath. I tried to ignore the sensation, but as the show went on I found it more difficult. There was no intermission, and when I went to the ladies' to have an attendant loosen my stays, the room was empty and I was given no choice…"

"No choice?' he questioned with a frown. "Did you go the course of Penelope and have someone cut the dress off for you in some deliciously savage manner?"

Flora pursed her lips for a moment before responding. "Well, almost."

"You little minx! Right there in the power room?"

"Hardly!" Flora gasped. "You know I'd never ruin a good silk."

"Practical of you."

"Now, will you let me finish?"

He nodded. "Proceed."

She rolled her eyes, but continued, nonetheless. "Well, I thought I would faint. The room was turning and I was so lightheaded. Seeing no other option, I had to give Andrew the task of…of loosening my stays." Flora hung her head, waiting for Charlie's response.

Instead of speaking, he merely burst out in uncontrollable chuckles, his neck and ears turning purple as he fought to control himself. Flora gave him several minutes to quit laughing, and when he did, he rasped out a faint, "My plan…my beautiful plan!"

"Your plan?"

Charlie wiped the tears from his eyes. "Yes, darling, my plan. Of course I thought it might end up being a tad more romantic than all that."

Flora blinked several times, almost too surprised for words. "How could you?"

"I'm the one who had the maid tighten that corset within an inch of your life, was I not?"

"Why would you do such a thing?" She stood from her seat, her hands planted on her hips. "I was mortified, Charlie!"

"But didn't it turn out in your favor? Isn't he going to call again?"

"Well, yes, but that's not the point! I didn't go to the opera with Andrew in hopes of him calling on me again."

"You didn't want him to return?" Charlie looked honestly confused. "I thought you rather liked each other."

"I'm in no state to entertain gentlemen."

"And why ever not?"

"I just think it's too soon," she whispered, sitting back down in her armchair. "After everything that happened I don't think I can do it all again."

"Flora, you don't have to be married tomorrow, or even speak to another man if you don't wish. But I hope that you make those decisions based on what you truly want and not what your broken heart tells you." Charlie's words rang truer than she would have liked to admit. "It won't hurt to go for a walk in the park with Andrew or out to dine."

"You called him Andrew." Flora giggled.

"Desperate times call for desperate measures. Now tell me what's on your mind so that I might help."

Flora debated opening up to Charlie. While his advice wasn't always good, he had never betrayed her confidence. Still, the thought of telling him her true thoughts was something she wasn't sure she was prepared to handle.

"It's nothing. I believe Conner and everyone will be here tomorrow morning. I should get back to my home and ensure that the staff has come and everything is prepared for their arrival." She readied herself to leave, calling for her coat and hat, which she pinned atop her head at a slight slant, just as Penelope had always instructed.

Charlie walked her to the door, making her pause before she stepped out into the cold. "You know you can always talk to me, Flora. I promise, I'm done giving you terrible advice. I've learned my lesson and I'm truly repentant."

"I know, and I will tell you everything…just not right now. I'm not really certain what I think, myself," she told him truthfully. "When I sort it all out, you'll be the first I talk to."

Charlie blew her a little kiss and sent her on her way. While her townhouse was several streets away, she needed the chilled air and long walk to clear her muddled mind. She hadn't given much thought to what her future plans were. She was merely concerned about the present, about hiding away as long as possible to escape her shame. Jasper had ruined her completely and thoroughly. He had used and abused her trust, taking away her maidenhead and leaving her an empty shell.

Flora knew deep down that she had gone willingly to his bed—seduced him, even. But she still felt as if that married man, who knowingly lied to her for years, had tricked her into it. It made her burn with anger and forced her skin to crawl in disgust. The entire affair had forced her to flee her home and find sanctuary in an empty house on the fashionable side of London.

She pulled her fur-lined cloak tighter round her neck as she walked slowly down the lanes toward home. But then a horse stopped beside her and it's rider jumped to the street. Flora was about to run; she had heard tales of highborn ladies being kidnapped for ransom, until she got a look at the rider's face.

"Andrew?"

He tipped his hat at her and gave her a dimpled grin. "Good afternoon, Flora. I was just on my way to your home. Are you in a hurry?"

"No, just walking."

He frowned. "No carriage? It's quite cold."

"I rather like the cold. It reminds me of Scotland." She then turned away and returned to her stroll, not sure how she could face him while her thoughts were drawn to her own ruin.

"Might I escort you?" he asked, holding tight to the rein of his horse.

"You don't have any previous engagements?"

"Nothing that can't wait to see you home.

Besides, seeing you *was* my engagement. Also, the sun will be down shortly."

"Ah, yes, the dangerous sunset," she retorted in a mock sinister voice. "There are lamps, you know."

He chuckled a bit. "Still, I don't mind the walk."

"Me either."

"Were you just seeing Charles?"

"Of course. I don't know many other people in London."

"You know me."

Flora smiled a bit, hoping the fur of her cloak hid her upturned lips. She was in no state to enter into matters of the heart, especially with someone as sweet as Andrew. She could feel his note burning against her breast as they walked and the ever gentle brush of his arm against her made her heart lurch in a peculiar manner she couldn't find a place for in her mind. Still, she found his presence oddly comforting, even in the silence. In fact, it was a rather companionable feeling, having him close, but quiet.

"So why were you coming to see me?"

"Flora, I know the opera didn't go quite as planned, but I hoped you might like to accompany me to a ball in few days' time?"

She felt her ears perk up. "A ball?"

"Why, yes. My uncle is having a gala in celebration of he and my aunt's wedding anniversary."

"Oh, how charming."

"It is. They've been married thirty years. Happily, I might add."

Flora glanced over at Andrew. His cheeks were

pink from the cold, and his hair gently tousled from the biting wind, but he didn't look bothered. "Thirty years…that's quite a feat."

"Yes. I hope that when I marry, it is as successful as their union." He turned toward her, a smile on his lips. "So, will you come with me?"

"Of course I will."

"Splendid! It's this Friday evening. I can come and collect you at seven, if that would be agreeable?"

"Very," she replied as they stopped before her townhouse. But she felt as if the conversation weren't over. "Andrew, my housekeeper has been working with the staff all day. Might you like to dine with me? It's almost time for supper."

He raised his brows. "I would like that very much." Then his gaze flew to his horse. "I suppose I should take him home?"

"No. Let me call for someone to see to your steed." Flora leisurely stepped up the stairs, keeping calm until she had entered the parlor, then ran frantically through the house, looking for Mrs. Neely. She found the woman in the kitchen, overseeing the portly cook. "Mrs. Neely, we're having a guest for supper and his horse needs attention."

"And when shall we expect your guest?" she asked, glancing up from the pot.

"He's here now." She knew the housekeeper wouldn't be pleased to see that Flora had brought a gentleman home, especially with such little notice.

But Mrs. Neely merely nodded then began barking out in Gaelic, causing a small boy to suddenly appear and zip past Flora to collect the horse. Then an old butler came to Flora's elbow and took her furs before leaving to find Andrew.

"Supper is simple tonight, my lady, is that all right?" the cook asked as she stirred the stew in her pot with one hand and kneaded dough with the other.

"I'm sure whatever you have prepared will be delicious," Flora answered. She then took a deep breath and stepped from the kitchen, pausing at a small mirror in the corridor. Carefully, she plucked the pins from her hat and put everything onto a side table where she was sure it would eventually be collected. She smoothed her hair a bit to tame the curls that had come out of her bun before stepping away to find her guest.

Andrew was in the drawing room, standing before the fire and peering intently at a painting of Flora's great, great grandfather spearing a boar. She paused in the doorway, clearing her throat softly to announce her entry. He jumped a bit and turned to her, wide-eyed, before straightening.

"Thank you for inviting me to dine. I hope it's no imposition?" he inquired politely.

"No, none at all." As she approached him, she felt a little uneasy in his presence. It was an odd sensation, as men had surrounded her all her life at the MacLeod keep. "I hope you don't mind that we'll dine rather simply this evening? The cook and the rest of the servants only just arrived this morning."

"You didn't travel with your help?"

"I left...quite suddenly. My brother and his wife

are coming tomorrow, and due to the wedding, there were too many servants to spare those that normally travel with us to London," she explained. "Charlie was kind enough to lend me one of his maids until my own from Scotland arrived."

"Then are you planning on staying long?"

Flora shrugged. "I haven't decided. I know that Drummond and Penelope will be coming through on their way home to Scotland, so I thought I might return with them."

The butler appeared in the open doorway. "Dinner is served in the dining room."

Andrew held out his arm for Flora to take, and the pair followed behind the butler. He helped her into her chair at one end of the long table, and then took his place at the second setting on the other side. Flora was a bit confused about the seating arrangements. They were so far apart, with a rather large fall floral arrangement plopped in the center of the oak tabletop. She leaned far to the left and only then could she see Andrew past the punches of orange blooms and decorative gourds.

"Lovely china!" he called, his voice echoing in the high ceiling.

"This is ridiculous," Flora spat. She rose from her seat and began gathering the plates and cutlery.

Andrew peered around a pumpkin and asked, "What are you doing?"

"We're so far apart, we can hardly speak without shouting. I won't let my voice grow hoarse when I could just move to sit beside you."

He stood and picked up his own glass and plate. "Don't trouble yourself, I'll move to you."

"Oh, don't fret. I've already gathered everything." But just as she said this, her bread plate fell to the floor and smashed into several pieces. She looked down at the shards and back up at Andrew, her eyes wide. "Oops."

The butler burst in the door. "What's happened? Miss Flora, are you all right?"

Flora choked back a laugh as she thought of how silly they must look; both she and Andrew had armfuls of flatware and balanced crystal goblets in their hands. "Quire well! We're just…rearranging out seats."

"Very well." The butler nodded, his face expressionless. "Please, allow me." He slipped the items from Flora's hands and set them on Andrew's right. Then the butler picked up the pieces of the plate and disappeared into the kitchen.

Andrew held out Flora's new chair before taking his own. They both stayed silent as the butler returned with two bowls and a replacement bread plate for Flora. A small team of footmen followed, each with a different dish.

The butler poured steaming beef stew for both of them, then piled their plates high with fresh fruit and steamed vegetables. Hot rolls, fresh from the oven followed, with pats of creamery butter. The team left without a word, leaving Flora and Andrew alone to dine.

"I do hope the fare isn't too simple for you," Flora began between bites. "Stew is a staple in Scotland. My mother says it warms the bones in cold weather."

"And I'll have to agree with her! This is

fantastic."

She smiled, pleased that he thought the meal satisfactory. "I'm glad you think so. This is one of my favorite recipes."

"Do you cook, Flora?"

"Me? Cook?" She giggled a bit. "That would be a dreadful idea. I don't know the first thing about it. I'd burn the house down."

"It's not as hard as all that."

"Are you trying to say that *you* cook?"

He smirked and speared a carrot with his fork. "Let's just say that I wouldn't starve if I were left to my own devices."

"Well, aren't you full of surprises?"

"What about you, Flora, what do you enjoy doing?"

Flora bit her lip, her mind wandering, unbidden, to her dalliance with Jasper. She shoved the thought away, throwing away the proverbial key. "Oh, this and that."

"That's a bit vague. Do you sew? Play an instrument, perhaps?"

"I do like to read. Mainly silly things like romances and mysteries."

"Mysteries?" Andrew raised his brows. "Have you had a chance to read *The Fog on the Lake*?"

She sat up straighter. "By T.R. Hamilton? No! I've been dying to get my hands on a copy, but there's none to be had in Scotland and all the copies were gone from The Piccadilly Emporium."

"That just won't do. I'll send you mine. I've finished it just yesterday."

"Oh, Andrew, thank you! It's the final in his

series, and I just have to know what happens!"

"Shall I tell you?" he teased. "Let you in on how it ends?"

"Goodness, no. That would be horrid."

He grinned mischievously and leaned toward her. "Aren't you a bit curious what becomes of the count and his captive?"

"Dreadfully so, but I won't let you spoil it." She laughed, tossing a roll at him.

It bounced against his chest and landed in his lap. He picked it up and took a bite. "Thank you, I needed another."

"Promise me, not another word about the count or his lighthouse or his poor dead wife!" She shook her finger at him. "I'll never speak to you again if you ruin this book."

"Quite passionate about your novels?"

"Only ones I like," Flora answered, pushing her plates away and ringing a bell for the help. When the butler and his lackeys arrived to clear their plates, Flora turned to the head of staff and said, "We'll take dessert and chocolate now, if you please."

"Anything else?" the butler questioned, peering at Andrew from under lowered brow.

"No, thank you," she replied, smiling sweetly up at him. When they were gone, she faced Andrew again. "He's always despised me."

"Who, your butler?"

She nodded. "Very much so. I was quite the wild child and he always hated how I would set the chickens free in the kitchen and steal the tarts as soon as they left the oven."

"What a brat." He laughed.

"A *noble* brat, which is the most terrible kind."

"It seems you've very much improved since then."

"I would hope so," she muttered as the butler returned with their treats. "Oh, goody, my favorite part of a meal."

She felt Andrew watching her as she piled their plates high with raspberry tarts, shortbread, and poured large cups of sweet hot chocolate. Flora tried to ignore his gaze. It churned her stomach to sense him so close, although they had been closer before. He watched her as she moved, but not like she was a specimen, but a piece of fragile art.

"Are you cold?" Andrew asked her, studying her face with his warm brown eyes. "You've suddenly gone pale."

"I'm fine, just a little tired," she lied smoothly.

She sipped her hot chocolate, waiting for the creamy sweetness to calm and cheer her. But it tasted like dust in her mouth and she fought to swallow the bitter stuff. And it wasn't that Andrew made her feel sick and unsettled. In fact, it was the opposite, and that frightened her greatly. He was gentle and sweet with noble ambitions and a jolly nature. And Flora was merely used goods.

Chapter Ten

Flora sat before the window, perking up as each carriage approached, then slumping back down when each passed the MacLeod town house. Conner and Charlotte were already several hours late in arriving, and she feared they had missed their train altogether. While she liked the freedom that came with no overbearing brother to vex her, she longed for his steady calm and Charlotte's warm embrace. Her courses still hadn't come and she was beginning to panic.

Thankfully, she had *The Fog on the Lake* to keep her company and her mind diverted. As soon as she saw it, she immediately opened the novel and hadn't put it down since. By the time she had awakened briskly at nine, the book was already waiting for her in the parlor. A small note accompanied it:

Flora,
I hope you find this book as enthralling as I find you. I look forward to discussing it at

length, at the ball.
  Yours,
  Andrew

She twirled the card between her fingers as she pored over the pages. The book was just as good as Andrew had promised, perhaps better. But the nagging thought of Charlotte and Conner never coming to London and leaving her to stew in her own ruination picked at her subconscious. She needed their amusing interactions to distract her and their strength to carry her through the tedious wait for her monthlies. Charlie was a well enough diversion, but he could only do so much. Besides, he was more likely to cause trouble than to soothe her.

When the familiar carriage stopped beside the walkway, she leaped from her seat and ran out the front door, knocking a poor footman to the side on her way. As soon as Conner left the carriage and held out his hand to help his wife, Flora threw her arms around his middle, breathing in the familiar woody, Scottish scent.

"Ach lass, ye scared the shite out o' me!" he roared with a wide grin, squeezing his sister.

"And you, a fearsome warlord." Charlotte giggled as she came to stand beside them, baby Alec in her arms.

"A year o' no one but my wee wife to fight with has left me soft." He sighed, patting his trim stomach.

Charlotte rolled her eyes and gave Flora a swift kiss before handing over her child into her sister-in-law's arms. "I see you're well?"

"Very," Flora answered, brushing a finger over Alec's chubby cheek. "But it's been too quiet without you two bickering and this little one to screech whenever he feels the need."

Alec yawned loudly in response and Flora gave him a peck on his little snub nose.

"Now ye've got the lad, he's your responsibility now."

Flora cooed down at her nephew. "Fine with me. He's precious."

"Aye, precious." Conner yawned and stretched. "Ye will no' think so in the wee hours o' the morning."

"Didn't you bring a wet-nurse?" Flora asked, handing Alec back to Charlotte, who took the boy inside.

"No, Charlotte believes in true motherin', as she did no' have one o' her own. How are ye, Flora?" He placed a heavy hand on her shoulder. "We've been worryin' about ye."

"I'm all right. Charlie's been keeping me entertained."

Conner grimaced, his jaw locking. "Lord, give me strength to no' throttle the fool."

"He's been on his best behavior." Flora turned and dashed up the stairs to evade the conversation and possible reprimand that was sure to follow. But before she entered the front door, she turned to look back at Conner and yelled, "Lovely to have you!"

***

Later, she found Charlotte lounging in the sitting room, Alec nowhere to be seen. "Where's the baby?"

"I gave him to Mrs. Neely to put down for a nap. He was very vexed to be taken from home."

The butler entered with a plate of sandwiches and tea.

"I'm so glad to be done traveling," Charlotte added.

"I was worried you missed your train."

She shook her head and took a bite of her food. "No, we actually saw Drum and Penelope just as we were on our way from the station."

"They're in London already?"

"Apparently so. I saw some footmen taking luggage into the Elmsly townhome."

"What about that place Drum was going to buy?"

She shrugged, taking another sandwich. "Apparently Penelope wanted to stay with her parents whenever they visit, as they won't see them any other time. Her parents are too old to travel far." Charlotte lay back on the arm of the couch, but shot up suddenly and reached between the cushions. She pulled out a small silver flask. "What on earth…"

Stifling a burst of laughter, Flora plucked the flask from her grip. "The rascal Charlie."

"Makes sense." She settled back. "Have you only seen him during your stay?"

"No…not exactly." Flora wasn't sure if she wanted to tell her sister-in-law about her evenings with Andrew. But after a moment of thought, she decided to keep it a secret. For now.

"Flora, you need to get out," Charlotte pressed gently. "It's no good to sit and dwell."

"I haven't been. I've had teas and even went to the opera house."

Charlotte smiled, her eyes closed. "I'm glad to hear it. But...is everything else...well?"

"What?"

She peeked at her through one eye. "Don't make me say it."

"Say what?"

"Your...*monthly*," Charlotte hissed.

Flora felt her stomach drop. With the excitement of seeing her family again, she had briefly forgotten about the importance of her courses. Without the regular reminder from her womb, she could still possibly be with child—Jasper's child. As she wracked her brain, she tried to remember the last time she had her monthly. It had never been important to her to track when it came. She clutched her middle, suddenly feeling very ill.

Charlotte sat up, her smooth brow uncharacteristically furrowed. "Don't fret, it'll be all right."

She groaned and unscrewed the lip of the flask, taking a heavy swig of whisky. "I'm embarrassed to admit that I was so focused on forgetting everything that transpired, that I forgot about *everything*."

"As you should have. I'm sorry for prodding. It was none of my business."

"No, I'm glad you've thought of it. I just don't believe I could handle carrying Jasper's child." Flora felt hot tears of fear and humiliation begin their long journey over the slopes of her cheeks.

"My heart would break."

Charlotte sighed and left her place, coming to kneel beside Flora. "Flora, what I am about to say to you is something out of love and my caring for you as my sister. What I will tell you is only for your ears and only to give you options you might not have known you had."

Flora wiped her face. "Options?"

She lowered her voice again. "There have been many, *many* women in high society who have found themselves…up the river, so to speak. Some go away for many months and return sadder and thick about the middle, always grieving, their children raised to never know their true parentage. Some bear the children and raise them as their own, always living in the shadow of their folly. Some give the baby to family, visiting often as an aunt or cousin. We could do that for you, if you wished it. Conner and I could take the child and give it the same life as Alec, with you to do as you pleased. I would never ask you to part with your child if that is not your wish." Charlotte paused and lowered her gaze. "And there is a final option."

"What is it?"

"I know of a woman…I've even sent some servants to her before, when they asked. She knows the brew that will keep the child from…she can relieve you of a pregnancy."

Flora felt as if she would faint, the horror of Charlotte's words chilling her to the bone. She would have never thought that her sister-in-law would suggest such a thing. "No."

Charlotte grasped her hands tightly. "I meant

nothing by it. You know I will help you in anything you choose to do in this world. All you need do is tell me how to help you and I will follow your instructions without question, nor judgment."

Flora felt the tears begin to flow again, the dampness followed by wracking sobs that shook her shoulders and scraped her throat raw. Everything that Charlotte had told her was monstrous in it's own way. She didn't feel she could bear to give her baby away, no matter whom the father was. But she also knew she couldn't raise it openly, as she could with one born in wedlock. The child would pay for her sins throughout its life by no fault of its own.

"Come," Charlotte fussed, drying Flora's cheek. "Let's get you into bed with some tea and a book. Would you like that?"

Flora sniffed. "Can you just bring me Andrew's book from the front room? I left it there when you arrived.

"Andrew? Andrew Philips?"

"He's a *friend* and he loaned me a novel in a series we both enjoy."

Charlotte pursed her lips, but her face was still almost unreadable. If she had any questions about the mysterious Andrew, she certainly wasn't going to ask at that moment. And Flora appreciated her sturdy resilience, thanking her good fortune to have Charlotte in her life.

It felt rather nice to be fussed over. Charlotte helped her out of her day dress and into bed, tucking the covers over her and around her legs. She then poured a cup of tea for Flora and splashed the remaining contents of Charlie's flask into the china for good measure. Lastly, she handed Flora *The Fog on the Lake*.

"Do you need anything else?" she asked as she twitched the bedroom curtains open just enough to let in some light for reading.

"No," Flora replied. "Thank you."

"Please, don't think of it." Charlotte went to leave, but then stopped at the door. "You know, Andrew has wonderful taste, and not just in books. You're a perfect darling, Flora, and anyone who thinks otherwise is a damned fool. Including you."

Flora stared at Charlotte until she left, and then kept her eyes on the closed door, her fingers soaking up the warmth of the teacup. She knew she meant well with her words, but they did little to calm her depression. Charlotte had wedded and bedded the love of her life and was now perfectly happy, as was Conner. Flora had done something wrong and lived to tell the tale.

She sipped her cooling tea and read her borrowed books. As she skimmed each line, a thought pricked the back of her subconscious. She imagined Andrew sitting before a fireplace, gripping the smooth leather spine of the novel, his slender finger keeping the pace. And when the tea was gone, the book read, and the last light of day gone from the window, Flora fell into a contented sleep, dreaming of a kind young man with a dimpled grin.

***

"Flora. Flora, get up," a voice cooed into her ear.

Flora pulled her comforter over her head and buried her face into the pillow. "Too early," she grumbled, trying to brush off the hand that was now shaking her shoulders. She felt the person sit by her side on the bed.

"Now, that's no way to treat your dearest friend."

She frowned. It sounded like something Charlie would say, but the voice was that of a woman. It could only be…"Penelope!" Flora threw off the blankets and flung her arms around Penelope's slender neck.

"Goodness, I can't breathe!" She laughed, holding Flora just as tightly.

"I'm so happy you're here." Flora heard her voice crack a bit as she spoke. "I've missed you so much and I want to hear everything about your trip! Oh, never leave again."

Penelope pulled away. "Don't fret. Drum can conduct his affairs from England or Scotland, so we can stay as long as we wish."

Flora's eyes flitted to the window, where bright light streamed in. "What time is it?"

"About noon. Charlotte said you were feeling poorly and wanted us to let you rest. But I couldn't wait any longer. I suppose you're exhausted from your evenings with Charlie, no doubt?"

"Yes, he and Andrew have kept me much entertained."

One of Penelope's fair brows lifted, as did the corner of her rosebud lips. "Well, there's a juicy bit of gossip I hadn't yet heard. I'm not sure how Charlie managed to keep it locked away when I saw him this morning."

Flora felt heat rise from her chest and burn the tips of her ears. "There's no gossip to be had."

Penelope pouted. "Well, that's not fair. You were privy to all my doings."

"Not *all* of them."

"Touché. Now, will you come down for luncheon? I know Drum will want to see you and I hope that I can pry a bit about your man from Charlotte if you won't talk."

"There's nothing to tell."

"Of course," she muttered in that even society voice she used with her mother, Cecily. Penelope then rose from the bed and went to the wardrobe, pulling out a pale yellow dressing gown. "Since you're ill, I don't have any qualms about you going down not fully dressed."

"I wasn't going to," Flora replied, pulling on the robe and tying the silk ribbon tight around her waist. "Do I look a fright?" She hadn't seen a mirror, but only assumed her face would be puffed and blotchy from the tears.

"Oh, Flora…" Penelope's gaze dropped to the ground. "I believe you should go bathe before coming to the dining room."

"What? Why?"

Penelope cleared her throat delicately and looked pointedly at the bed. Flora followed her gaze and saw something she had been praying to see for two weeks. Her courses had come. There would be no child.

***

"Finally, there're the lasses!" Drummond bellowed as Flora and Penelope entered the dining room. He immediately crossed to them and pulled Flora into a tight embrace that lifted her feet from the ground. "So good to see ye. Are ye in good health?"

Flora smiled. "I feel *so* much better," she told him in all honesty. It felt as if a great weight had been lifted off her chest.

Drummond set her back down and went to help his wife into her seat. Flora took hers beside Charlotte, who looked at her rather strangely.

"You seem in good spirits," Charlotte pointed out as their food was brought in.

"Because I have a lot to be happy about." Flora tucked a strand of still-damp hair behind her ear and leaned toward her, lowering her voice. "I awoke to my courses."

Charlotte let out an audible sigh. "This *is* good news."

"Very much so. It is as if I've gotten a second chance at life."

"What are ye whisperin' about over there?" Conner questioned from the other side of the table.

"Charlotte's taking me shopping for a new gown," Flora lied smoothly, straightening up.

"A new frock?" Conner grimaced. "Ye have closets full o' dresses."

"But not one of deep blue," Charlotte pointed out as she stirred her steaming bowl of soup.

Conner made a Scottish sound in his throat. "Ye lie, wife. I know right well that the lass has several. I get the bills, ye ken?"

"But do you have any of *sapphire* blue?" Penelope asked, looking particularly thrilled to be speaking about shopping.

Flora thought about the few gowns she had brought to her when she fled to London. "No...I have a green, a pink, some blue...but not one of that particularly royal shade."

"Perfect. I looked in on my father's emporium and he has some lovely silks, thanks to Drum's gift." Penelope gazed up at her husband with such unmasked adoration, Flora felt like an interloper into their short moment.

"That settles it then," Charlotte announced. "We'll go find Flora a dress this afternoon. Perhaps for the New Year feast we're having back at the castle?"

"Why this afternoon? Can't it wait a bit?" Conner asked.

Flora turned up her nose. "Well, I need a new dress for Friday."

"What's Friday?" Penelope's voice was innocent, but Flora knew she was waiting for a hint.

"Andrew is taking me to a ball his uncle is hosting."

Conner opened his mouth as if to say something, then snapped it shut. Flora could tell he wanted to know more about Andrew, probably so he could spy on the poor man. Although she had no right to feel anything toward Andrew, she felt as if she should shield him from Conner. If her brother had been protective before, she knew he could double down on his resolve to keep her safe from harm by a man's hands. And Flora wasn't looking forward to seeing how his concern would manifest.

Chapter Eleven

Penelope dabbed at Flora's cheeks with her red-coated fingertip.

"Just a touch of rouge," she said. "Too much and you'll look like a harlot...or as if you have some dreadful illness."

Flora brushed off the intrusive thought that 'harlot' was an adequate word to describe her. Instead of giving in, she began digging through her jewelry box atop the dressing table and put on some heavy pearl earrings and a matching choker that she hoped would lengthen her neck.

"Those go well with the silks," Penelope told her, closing up the jar of rouge. "I'm glad we decided on this blue striped gown. Rather more interesting than the ones without a pattern."

"You don't think it strange?" Flora felt the dress suited her, but she didn't wish to stand out too much.

"I was just in Paris and I know for certain that stripes are in the height of fashion."

"I do hope you're right." Flora stood and stepped

into her slippers. "I'm glad that gloves are no longer the fashion. I've always hated them."

"Truth be told, so did I. I have a pair of spectacular hands and it's a pity that they had to stay hidden."

Flora giggled and took one last look in the mirror before following Penelope out of her bedchambers. Andrew was already standing in the parlor, his face white and his mouth a firm line. At first, Flora wondered if he were ill. But when she reached the landing, she saw Conner leaning against the doorway of the sitting room, polishing his already clean dirk with a faded piece of flannel.

"Aye," Conner said evenly with a nod, his eyes set on Andrew's frozen frame. "This wee blade has butchered many a hog. I've even used it to castrate some o' my animals. Do ye ken much about castration, Philips?"

"No, my lord, I can't say that I do." Andrew's voice was deep and clear, but Flora suspected he was much more frightened than he let on.

"Well, I'd be more than happy to show ye how—"

Flora placed her balled hips upon her hands. "Conner, this is not the time nor the place for you to be doing this. We all know you're compensating with that ridiculous knife."

"Ach, lass." Conner chuckled. "Philips and I were just gettin' to know each other. Isn't that right, Philips?"

She rolled her eyes and brushed past Penelope, who was watching the goings-on with unveiled amusement. "Are we ready to go, Andrew?"

"Yes," he said, putting on his hat. "The carriage is outside."

"Lovely." Flora put on her cloak and looked over her shoulder at Conner. "Goodbye. I'll possibly be late, so don't fret."

Conner muttered something in Gaelic. She could barely hear him, but she did hear the words, "kill," "fancy lad," and "join a convent." She ignored him and stepped out into the cold night air. The first inhale chilled her lungs, but she smelled snow and the possibility of seeing the white powder covering the busy city of London thrilled her. It was even more true since it was still late fall, which only ever held the eventual promise of snow.

Once they were settled in the carriage, Flora allowed herself to relax. But she noticed that Andrew sat poker straight, his hands folded in his lap.

"I hope Conner didn't abuse you thoroughly."

"Not at all. He just spoke to me of the joys of wielding the broadsword and how he once hung a man for mishandling a woman in a nearby village."

Flora groaned. "I'm so sorry. How humiliating."

"It's quite all right. I've never been threatened by a laird before. Rather novel experience." He grinned. "Thankfully, there will be so many people at my uncle's, no one should pay us any mind and I won't be tempted to share my new knowledge about castration."

Flora had put a great deal of effort into her dressage, and it would be a pity if no one took in her fabulous gown. Come to think of it, Andrew hadn't said a word about her looks since she found him on the landing, looking white as a ghost. She crossed her arms and decided to give him some time to get over being threatened with bodily harm by Conner before she added her own hidden dirk to the mix.

Andrew's uncle's home was a fine manor, tucked into the edge of London. Lanterns lighted the front gardens and men in white livery helped them from the carriage the moment it stopped before the wide front doors. She took Andrew's arm and allowed a maid to take her furs as she looked about at the fine gathering before her. She noticed several ladies from the season before, her first in London. But they were all married now, many sporting baby bumps, hidden by the folds of their fashionable gowns. Flora placed a hand on her own flat stomach, momentarily thankfully she wouldn't be in their position until she was truly prepared.

"Champagne, sir?" a butler asked Andrew, offering him his pick from a silver serving tray. "And for your wife?"

"Oh!" Flora felt her cheeks heat. "We're not—"

"Thank you." Andrew passed her a glass before taking one for himself. "Cheers, *wife*."

Flora giggled. "Cheers, husband." She clinked her class to his before taking a sip.

"Look, the snow's begun." He nodded upward to the domed skylight above the ballroom, which was frosted with the newly fallen flakes. "I hope it doesn't impede our journey home. But of course if it does, my uncle will be sure to host us for the night."

"I love snow," Flora murmured, a faint childlike

feeling building in her breast. "When we were young, all us girls would mistreat Conner most horribly. He'd be out with our father training, and we'd throw snowballs at him from the balcony above. Then we'd hide from him in the secret cubbies."

"Secret cubbies?"

"The castle is full of them. There are tunnels, trap doors, and concealed chambers. Conner thinks he knows them all, but I know for her certain there are at least three he isn't aware of."

"How marvelous!" he exclaimed, drawing closer. "Are the hidden places a new addition? Or were they there from the moment of construction? How many secret corridors are there? Do people get lost within them?"

Flora laughed at his enthusiasm. "I'm not sure when they came to be. I'm assuming they're from all different times. The MacLeod keep was originally built around 900 AD, but there have been many expansions and renovations since then."

"How I'd love to get my hands on a map."

"Conner has several in his study in Scotland. I'm sure he wouldn't be adverse to allowing you a look."

"Are you inviting me to Scotland?" he asked with an air of pretend innocence.

Flora drained her glass. "You're a fool. No one wants to go to Scotland, even the Scots! We're a dying breed."

"And who told you such nonsense?"

"The headmistress at the Chesterfield School for Ladies."

"Isn't that in York, England?"

She nodded at an older woman she recognized from Penelope's wedding before turning back to Andrew. "Yes, all my sisters and myself were educated there. My mother thought it better than being taught by a tutor at the castle."

"Ah, I always wondered why you didn't have an accent."

"I do…but only when I'm angry," she confided with a wink.

"And what makes you angry?"

"When I'm invited to a ball by a gentleman, and he neglects to ask me to dance."

"On your orders." He gave both of their cups to a passing footman and drew Flora to him, pulling her toward the twirling couples.

She laughed as he flung her about, much to the disgrace of the other dancers. "You didn't even properly ask me!"

"Too late for that now, I think."

Andrew wasn't a refined dancer. He lacked the simple grace that many of the men possessed as they followed the correct steps at the correct moments. But he had a certain lightless on his feet and as he spun her about the room, they both laughed loudly with delight. Normally, she would have found the simple pleasure of a finely executed dance enjoyable, but Andrew's wide dimpled grin and his hands on her waist made her wish that every dance could be so good for the rest of her life.

She panted as they came to a stop several songs later, by the edge of the crowd. She had dropped her fan somewhere during their fun, and she wished she had it then. Andrew looked a bit flushed a well. He passed her a glass of iced punch before drinking two in succession.

Flora's gaze drifted around the room toward an open side door, where she could see drifts of snow. "Andrew, how would you like to cool down the Scottish way?"

His auburn brows rose. "The Scottish way?"

"Come." She grabbed him by the sleeve of his jacket and pulled him through the throngs of people and out to the doorway. She inhaled a deep breath and shivered a bit as a light breeze brushed her face. The sight of untouched virgin snow in the darkened gardens was almost magical. It glowed in the light of the full moon.

"Yes, the fresh air feels nice."

She lifted the hem of her gown to keep it from growing damp, feeling the goose bumps rise up her legs and prick her bare arms. "It's lovely."

"What are you doing?" he asked from behind her. "You'll catch your death out here."

"Nonsense. I'm a Scot. We thrive in the cold," she retorted, taking her first steps into the pristine snow. Each one made a delightful crunch beneath her slippers. Flora was glad the snow wasn't too deep, as she was sure it would freeze her feet right through her shoes and stockings.

Andrew shifted from side to side, glancing over his shoulder at the brightly lit ballroom. "Flora, where you going?"

"Come on, Andrew, we'll be the first people to ever touch this snow."

"I can't return you to your brother sick. He'll

stab me or have be pulled apart by wild horses."

Flora pouted and dropped her dress, letting the hem touch the white sheet below. "He'll be even more cross with you if I wander off in a blizzard alone and die."

"This isn't a blizzard," he told her, stamping over to meet her. "The snow is barely falling now."

"But isn't it marvelous?" Flora lifted her eyes toward the sky, watching each tuft fall down from the heavens. "It reminds me of home."

"It is marvelous." Andrew wasn't looking at the sky, but at Flora.

From the corner of her eye, she watched him observe her. He was studying her, but not like a specimen as some British girls did, and not like a fine meal as Jasper had, but like something delicate and beautiful—a glass vase or porcelain statue. She barely felt the snow grazing against her cheeks until a warm brush of fingers brought her face toward his.

Andrew stood before her, his palm gently cupping her jaw. Flora closed her eyes, involuntarily leaning into his touch. Then his free hand found one of hers and he intertwined their fingers. She wanted to open her eyes, to look at the man who had shown her such unconditional kindness and understanding. But she was afraid—afraid of hoping for something that could never be, afraid of what their locked gazes could do, afraid of him seeing what she really was beneath the silks and pearls.

"Flora," Andrew started quietly. "Please, look at me."

She forced herself to follow his instruction. His hair had been tousled by the wind and snowflakes clung to his lashes. Flora found it hard to keep her eyes on his. Instead, she allowed her gaze to drift over his face, which was dimly lit by the full moon, making his features seem more rugged and strong. He had always been a handsome man, but at that moment, she didn't think she had ever seen anyone more striking.

Andrew took a deep breath. "Flora, I know that my feelings toward you aren't exactly hidden. But I still feel the need to say them aloud."

She felt her breath leave her body. "Andrew, I—"

"Just listen to me," he pleaded. "I know that talking is your particular specialty and hobby, but if I don't speak now, I fear I never will."

She merely nodded, focusing on the steady warmth of his hands.

"I am not a duke, nor a lord, but I *will* be a barrister. My uncle's made it clear that he's going to have me take over his London practice next month. It will be fully my business and responsibility."

Flora bit her lip. Andrew was starting a new life and while she was pleased for him, her kind had no place in his world. "Congratulations. That's very exciting." She tried to force a smile, but her mouth felt dry and her wounded heart wouldn't allow her face to obey.

"I'm not finished. I will never be titled or own a castle, but I'd give you a good life, Flora. A life of mystery novels and dancing and dresses and standing in the snow like utter fools because it reminds you of Scotland." He released her, then drew his hand around her waist, pulling her against him. She could almost feel the strong beating of his heart beneath the palm of her hand, which now rested upon his breast. "I know that Scotland will always be where you're from, but I would like your home to be with me."

He dipped down then and pressed his lips to hers. The motion was soft and tender and warmed Flora to the bones. She leaned hungrily into his mouth and threw her arms about his neck. The soft caresses of skin were nothing like the kisses she had before. There was a different kind of longing that spread through her body, not one of lust, but one of grasping need that felt as necessary as air. They melded into one being, protected and preserved in a sea of falling snow.

When he pulled away, Flora felt almost lightheaded, floating in a sea of haze.

"I don't know the ways of women or any honey coated words of wooing, but I know that I care for you so deeply. Flora, it might be a little late to ask this...but I would like your permission to court you. I want to make my intentions with you known and go about things the proper way."

"Your intentions?" she asked, content to stay in the snowy bubble they had created.

"Yes, my intentions to one day marry you."

"*Marry* me?" Flora shrieked, twisting out of his arms. "No!"

Andrew blinked several times. "Well...not this moment, no...but with the law practice and your brother being in London...I thought..." He ran his fingers through his hair then suddenly straightened his posture, his face unreadable. "I'm so dreadfully sorry that I misinterpreted our time together. Your gown is wet and it is very cold outside. I'll accompany you home, presently."

Flora watched, mouth agape, as he turned on his heel and stalked toward the house. She rationally knew that she had no place to be cross with him for his frostiness, but it stung nevertheless. Flora was stunned by his sudden coldness, and without his close proximity, she felt the dampness of the snow seep in through her gown and stockings, chilling her. He waited for her at the door, then hurried her around the edge of the ballroom and toward the front to collect they coats.

When they were seated in the carriage, Andrew finally looked her way, frowning as she shivered. He drew off his overcoat and draped it over her legs without a word. Then he turned his attention back to the window. Flora knew she had hurt him by her sudden dismissal of his declaration. She couldn't have him suffering over her own shortcomings, or worse, allow his affection to continue and saddle him with an unworthy wife. Either way, there would be pain.

"Andrew?" she asked timidly.

"Yes, Flora?"

"I need to explain—"

"No need. I understood you perfectly."

She grimaced. "That's not what I meant. Just listen to be me, please. I didn't respond so because I don't care for you. It's *because* I care that I said those things."

He sighed, lines appearing between his brows. "Flora, what do you mean? Is it because I'd have to live in London? Would you miss Scotland so much? We could visit as often my schedule allows." Andrew looked so sincere as he spoke.

"It's not that." Flora heard her voice crack with unshed tears. The carriage then stilled by the front doors of the MacLeod townhome, but neither moved to get out. "It's only…oh, Andrew!" She buried her face in her hands. "I just can't!"

He pulled her hands away and held them tightly in his own. "Why can't you, Flora, if you care for me?"

Tears streamed down her cheeks, but Flora didn't move to wipe them away. "Because I'm no good for you, Andrew."

"How can you say what's good for me?" He raised his voice. "I'm an educated man, Flora. I'm capable of knowing what's good for me and knowing what I want. And what I want now and forever is *you*."

"I, I…I can't, I'm sorry. I can't let you!" she cried, yanking her fingers from his grasp and pushing his coat from her lap and onto the floor between them.

"Flora, please…"

"I'm sorry," she whispered before throwing open the carriage door and jumping in a pile of slush that had been created by the passing carts. She scrambled through the snow and ice to the front door, which opened just as she reached for the knob.

"Flora, wait!" Andrew called out. He had slipped

and fallen upon his own dismount and was unable to get his footing in the snow.

"What in the bloody world is this?" Conner bellowed, pulling Flora inside by the arm and slamming the door shut behind them. "Bring me my blade!" He yelled to no one in particular.

"No, don't!" Flora sobbed. "He didn't do anything wrong!"

"Then why are ye soaked to the bone and cryin' so, home from a party hours early?" He looked around at the entry wait. "I said for someone to be me my blade!" he shouted again.

"Flora? Flora?" Andrew called from the other side of the door as he pounded his fist against it. "Please, Flora, speak to me!"

"That bastard," Conner growled, pushing up the sleeves of his shirt. He was about to open it when Flora threw herself before him.

"Conner, listen to me. He's done nothing wrong. All he wants to do is court me, but I can't do it." Flora wiped at her eyes. "I can't."

"And he would no' take no for an answer?"

"It's not that...he just...he's so kind and likes me so."

Conner stood there, aghast, for a moment. "All this because that lad *likes* ye?"

Charlotte rushed in, wearing a dressing robe with a sword in her hands. "What's going on?" Then she saw Flora seated on the floor before the door and her hazel eyes widened. "Flora! Are you all right?"

"Yes," she sobbed in response.

"Flora, I can hear you!" Andrew called out. "And I know you can hear me. I know you're safe, so I'll go home now. But please, think about what I said. It's all I ask."

She cried harder when she heard the sound of his carriage leaving—loud, raking sobs that made her throat sore. Conner exchanged glances with Charlotte before picking Flora up and carrying her up the stairs and to her bedroom. When he had sat her upon the trunk at the foot of her bed, he kissed her gently on the forehead. When he turned to leave, he paused for a moment, as if to say something, but then left her in the capable hands of his wife.

Charlotte leaned the broadsword against the bed and began tending to her patient silently. She took off Flora's furs and ruined slippers. Then she helped her out of her dress and stays and stockings, taking off her pearls last, leaving Flora in a damp shift.

"Shall you have a nice bath?" Charlotte asked in a voice that was just above a whisper. "You're so cold." Just as she said this, two maids arrived. One carried wood and began to build the fire higher. The other carried a covered tray in one hand and a hot water bottle in the other.

"I think I'd just like to get into something dry and get into bed," Flora answered as the one maid began drawing back her covers and tucking the heated water bottle within.

Charlotte pulled out a fresh nightgown for Flora, and once she was dressed, pulled the blankets well over her body. "Are you warm enough?"

Flora wiggled her toes, which felt admittedly better. "Yes, just starving now."

"Poor duck didn't even have supper?" Charlotte

lifted the top of the tray the maid left. "It seems Conner sent you up some tea and a bit of the stew we had for dinner."

She breathed in the comforting smell and began eating as soon as Charlotte put the tray on her lap. The food warmed her frozen body and nourished her bruised heart. She tried to keep her thoughts from Andrew, instead focusing on counting each pin Charlotte plucked carefully from her hair. But by the time the pins were all gone, the thoughts of Andrew still remained.

"I will not ask you what happened," Charlotte said as she took the empty tray and dimmed the oil lamp beside Flora's bed. "But I will ask you, what will you do now?"

"I don't know," she replied.

"Well, what do you *want* to do?"

"I want to go home."

Chapter Twelve

The train trundled past more rolling hills, their white tops glowing orange in the morning light. Flora leaned back into her velvet seat and clutched her plaid wrap tighter around her shoulders. She thought it strange how as soon as she stepped onto the train, she was shedding one part of herself for the other. When she left Scotland, she discarded her tartan and loose locks in favor of lace shawls and hairpins. And when she left England, she no longer wore her feathered hats and silk slippers and instead picked up her plaid and a pair of sturdy shoes for trekking the rocky slopes along the Scottish sea.

Flora had to wait two days to get her ticket for the train home. The snow had to be cleared, and a private cabin secured for her use. So for two whole days she laid in bed, ignoring Andrew's cards and flowers. She couldn't bear to tear open the small envelopes, so she had tied them with a ribbon and tucked them safely into her traveling case. She knew that she should have sent him word of her leaving, but found that she couldn't bear the thought

146

of telling him goodbye.

She heard a knock on her sliding door. Thinking it the breakfast she ordered, she rose and pulled it open to find Drummond standing in the corridor.

"Mornin', Flora. Can I come in?"

"Of course." She stepped aside and allowed him entry. They sat on either side of the cabin.

"How are ye?" he asked, looking out the window. "We should be there in a few hours, but I wanted to see that ye were well."

"Fine," she replied. "Where's Penelope?"

He waved his large hand. "Ye know her. Can no' be seen without dressin' up, or some such thing."

There was another knock on the door and a woman entered pushing a cart laden with tea, bacon, sausage, eggs, toast, potatoes, and biscuits. She left it between them, disappearing as quickly as she had come.

"Finally," Flora sighed, immediately biting into a piece of bacon.

"That's quite a breakfast. Did ye order for three?"

She rolled her eyes. "I can't have a full English breakfast?"

"But why so much?" Drum asked as he speared a sausage with his dirk and took a bite.

"Oh, yes, of course you can eat my food," she said sarcastically as he took some toast.

"Ye can no' eat all this, ye'll pop like a tick."

"Who cares if I get fat? All the proper spinsters are," she explained, her mouth full of food. "I'm rather looking forward to not having to watch my figure as I raise a lovely heard of poodles."

"And when have ye ever watched your figure?"

"I just want to drown my sorrows in fried eggs and pork. Is that so terrible?"

Drum nodded. "Aye. Aye, I think it is."

"And why is that?"

"Because I know how ye feel and I know ye feel like shite."

Flora put down her fork and took a sip of tea. "I feel *fine*."

Drum draped his arms over the tops of the seats. "Ye know, I remember a few months ago that you and I sat in a train cabin, much like this one."

"Oh, no," she sighed, her appetite gone.

"Oh, aye," Drum replied with a grin. "Ye sat where I do now, tellin' me what a fool I was bein'. You shook your wee finger at me and said that leavin' Penelope in London was the worst thing I ever did and I would regret it the rest o' my life."

"And now you're happily wed. Yes, I know," she muttered, crossing her arms over her chest.

"Why can ye no' do the same? He's from a good family, no' titled, but a hard worker. And from what I've heard, he's right fond o' ye."

"He asked me to…well, not to marry him, but to be in a courtship and…"

"And what?"

Flora leaned her head against the window, her breath fogging up the glass. "I just couldn't."

"Do ye no' fancy the lad? What's wrong with him?"

"Nothing. He's smart, good looking, kind, funny when he cares to be, and he promised to give me everything in his power to give."

"Then what happened, Flora?"

Tears pooled in her eyes, but she blinked them away. "I can't tell you."

"Ye can tell me anythin', lass. We've always been honest with one another, maybe to a fault. Hell, your meddlin' in my business is what got me Penelope."

"You'll judge me," she whispered.

Drum stood and pushed the cart aside, coming to sit beside Flora. "I'll no judge ye, nor betray your secrets. Even to my wife, unless what ye tell me could be o' harm."

"I...well, you know...you know Jasper..."

"That arsehole? What o' him?"

Flora cringed. "Well, have you heard he's been banished?"

Drum scratched his chin. "Aye, I've heard he wronged his wife, or somethin' o' the like. I did no' know he even had one. But I do no' know the particulars o' what he did."

"And no one will, thanks to Conner."

His green eyes narrowed. "Did he hurt ye, lass?"

"Not like you think. For years he's been flirting with me and I thought he would...that he might.... I thought we'd be married. Conner didn't approve of my ideas and I thought that...well..." She closed her eyes as she felt the heat of her embarrassment burn her skin.

"Oh, lass, ye did no'," Drum groaned, hanging his head.

"I did."

"Why would ye do such a thing?"

"It worked for you and Penelope. I thought it

would be the same for Jasper and I."

"But how did Conner come to find this out? Don't tell me he caught ye…in the act?"

Flora smiled wryly. "I didn't go as far as you did and traipse around in my dressing gown."

"Then what happened?"

"I went to Conner and told him everything, then demanded to be wed. He exploded. I was locked in my rooms and the next day they brought Jasper's wife in and…well, I went to London to grieve with Charlie and we kept bumping into Andrew, who helped me to bed after your wedding. I was very drunk and Una…well, Una was seducing Jasper, and Andrew had a stutter and now he doesn't and now I'm…here."

"Well, I did no' understand much o' that, but I'm failin' to see why you are cross with Andrew."

"I'm *not* cross with him, and that's the problem."

"Then tell me what is so we can stop goin' about in circles."

Flora turned to him. "Can't you see what's wrong?"

"No, I can no'."

"How?" Flora was exasperated. She didn't wish to say aloud that she was a ruined woman.

"Ye care for him, he cares for ye, and Conner does no' have any issue with the match."

She hid her face in her hands. "I'm ruined."

"What did ye say? I can no' year ye when your mouth is covered."

"I'm no longer a maid," she whispered through her fingers.

"Is that all?"

Flora looked up at him, perplexed. "Did you hear me?"

"Aye. And I'll have ye know, I was no' a *maid* when I bedded Penelope."

"But you're a man! It's different for you," she cried, thumping a fist upon her thigh.

"Perhaps, but she did no' think so. And I would have still loved her if she had no' been one."

"But Andrew is a true gentleman. He could never accept this."

"Have ye asked him?"

Flora gasped. "And tell him what I did? Of course not!"

"Is he so simple and soft that ye can no' trust him?"

"No, that's not it."

"Then you're scared?"

His words were simple, but true. She *was* scared. The thought it rejection and shame frightened her. "I am. But now I'm going home and it's over now."

"Did ye even tell him ye were leavin'?"

Flora's cheeks warmed. "Not exactly."

"Then he'll knock on the door today and Conner will answer and tell him what?"

"That I've gone home."

"Ach, at least I said goodbye to Penelope when I left."

"Ouch."

He patted her knee. "I know it hurts, but ye need someone to tell ye what you're doin' is wrong."

"Do you really think so?"

"Aye, I do." He stood. "I have to get back to Penelope now. And I think ye should find a way to

151

get back to Andrew. As a wise Scottish lass with a big, loud mouth once told me, ye do no' simply find a love like that and let it slip through your fingers. But if ye do, ye never deserved it anyway. And, Flora, I've known ye since birth. Ye are my blood and my kin and ye deserve a great love."

***

"Flora!" Gwen burst from the doors of the MacLeod keep as soon as the line of carriages came to a halt.

Flora grinned as her curly haired sister pulled her into a hug the moment her feet landed on Scottish ground. "Oh, Gwen, I've missed you so terribly."

"I had no idea you were coming back! Wee Ian was out riding with Big Angus and they saw your carriages."

"Still, how did you know it was us?"

"Who else would be coming?" Gwen giggled then shrieked when Drum swooped in behind her and lifted her into a bear hug. "You two are back as well?"

"When Flora said she was leaving, it just made sense to accompany her," Penelope explained. "Besides, we needed to ensure that all was well with our home."

"Then are you leaving right away?" Gwen pouted prettily as soon as Drum put her down.

Flora pulled her plaid tighter around her shoulders as a gust of wind tore through them. "No, they're going to stay on a few days. But can we go inside? It's freezing."

"Oh! Of course!" Gwen hooked her arm into Flora's and leaned in close. "Has something happened? I thought I wouldn't see you until the New Year."

"I'll explain everything in due time. I just want to get into a bath and wash the scent of travel off me."

The girls walked up the stairs into Flora's bedchambers, where Gwen quickly ran a bath, fragrant with orange blossoms. Once she was undressed, Flora gratefully dipped into the water. But she was only allowed a few moments of peace before Gwen began sighing and tapping her shoe expectantly.

"Please stop that," Flora begged. She debated holding her head under the water, merely to avoid the impending conversation, but feared that drowning would be a rather unattractive way to die.

"You know that I can't."

"Why is it that we always have these types of conversations while I'm in the bath?"

"Because you can't run away," Gwen said simply. "Now, tell me everything. Even just the condensed version will do."

Flora took a breath, suddenly feeling exhausted. "Might we have this conversation another day? I'm just so tired of thinking about it. Please, just let me think of other things."

She frowned, but asked nothing more of London. "Well, wee Ian has taken in a pregnant barn cat, much to the maids' dismay. Cook is also planning a large feast this year for Martinmas."

"Is it already November? My, time has passed."

"Drum and Penelope were married two nights before Samhain, remember?"

"Oh, yes. With everything going on, it must have slipped my mind."

"So be prepared to help with the black pudding this year. Some of the maids left the castle, and Cook doesn't know if she can get new girls in beforehand to help in the preparations."

Flora thought that odd. It was rare that a maid left MacLeod keep unless it was to be married. Conner always ensured they were paid well and were kept housed and generally happy. "Why did they leave?"

Gwen averted her eyes and paused a moment before replying. "Well, I suppose it's better you hear it from me…it seems that Jasper had sown his wild oats a bit more than we thought. When he left, several maids left as well out of the shame of his wife appearing and all that. One was with child."

"Goodness," she murmured, wishing she had left Gwen behind when she went for a bath.

"Yes, so we're a tad shorthanded. I was going over the accounts and—"

"The accounts?"

"Yes, you know I've always had a head for numbers. I asked Conner if I could practice with the accounts here. It's something that will come in handy when I'm married and will be a great help when I must run my own household. I know you wouldn't have noticed, but I have been in charge of the accounts for a number of months now."

Flora's brows rose at Gwen's nonchalance. "You know, I've never heard you speak of the future. It's quite odd, now that I reflect upon it."

"I'm eighteen now. I suppose marriage is something that I should begin thinking about. Being able to run a household is an attractive skill to most men."

"Gwendolyn, do you have a suitor?" Flora asked with a wide smile. "Who is it?"

Gwen rolled her eyes. "I'm allowed to pick up useful talents without having a particular man in mind."

"Well, that's no fun. But still, tell me how you're finding your work."

"It's easier than I thought it would be. I just keep track of the household, the deliveries, the trades, and I'll be marking down the taxes over the coming days, if Conner isn't back soon enough to oversee it."

"That's a lot of responsibility."

"It keeps me busy. I like the quiet and the stillness of numbers. Besides, no one bothers me when I appear very busy and I rather like not being bothered with to go sew with the other ladies and such. But I *am* having a bit of trouble with something."

"What is it?"

"There's one Spanish ship we do trade with, several times a year. They bring us things from the south and east, usually spices, rice, tobacco…several things. Well, it seems as if they have been shorting us, costing the treasury a good deal of money."

Flora thought to the fragrant Indian tea she loved and the beautiful ivory bracelets she had received

155

for her last birthday. Forgoing those exotic pleasures would make her very unhappy. "But if we stop trade with them, how will we get those things?"

"On the recommendation of one of Baron Elmsly's friends, I've sent word to a Portuguese trader last month at his home port, as soon as I had severed ties with the Spanish ship. I hope he gas gotten my message with the new orders, or we'll be without some of our creature comforts for a time."

"I'm sure all will be well."

"I as well. He sails the…oh, what is it called?" Gwen bit her lip and Flora could almost see her mind at work as she thought. "Oh, *A Sereia* I believe."

"What?"

"*A Sereia*," she repeated slowly. "It's Portuguese for…dolphin, perhaps? I can't recall."

"You don't know?"

Gwen scoffed. "I speak French and German, not Portuguese."

"Oh, my mistake." She giggled before wringing the soap from her hair. "Hand me a towel and my robe, please."

Gwen held out both, and when Flora was dry and wrapped tightly, she sat before the fire to brush her tangled hair. Her sister took the seat opposite and pulled her feet up, wrapping her arms around her knees. Flora watched Gwen as she peered into the flickering flames of the fire. She knew her sister was dying to know what happened, but respected her wishes to have one night of peace.

"Do you think it's time for dinner, then?" Flora

asked once her hair was relatively tame. "I miss Scottish food."

"You were gone less than two weeks."

"Two weeks without Scottish food is a long time. Now help me dress so we can go find something to eat."

***

No one was aware of what had happened between Flora and Jasper. Although she knew this, when she and Gwen strode into the feasting hall, she felt everyone watching her. It was almost as if everyone present was judging her. Of course everyone had always watched when she entered a room, but that night, it felt different.

"You're white as a ghost," Gwen murmured as they took their seats at the head table.

"Just tired," she lied, plastering a smile upon her lips as maids and footmen began milling about the room with plates of food.

Her gaze strayed toward Jasper's group of friends. They were more somber and controlled than before, when their ringleader was around to goad them into drink. She waited to see if any looked her way—if they blamed her for their friend's disappearance—but none did. They ate, drank, laughed, and talked as they always had. Flora knew no one was really watching her, but she felt uneasy all the same.

Gwen was watching her out of the corner of her eye and pushed her cup toward her. "Drink."

"What is it?"

"Just drink it."

"I don't want to," Flora told her, ripping her roll in half.

"Just a bit," Gwen pressed in a baby voice. "One teensy sip for me?" She batted her long eyelashes as her mouth split into a little grin. "It'll help."

Flora warmed a bit at Gwen's amusing manner. Having such a playful sister was always so uplifting. It always surprised everyone that she was the shyest and quietest of all the MacLeod girls. But Flora knew better. Her little Gwen was the most wild of the bunch when out of the company of strangers.

She lifted the goblet to her lips and took a long swallow. It tasted bitter and nothing like the soothing honey she was used to. "Gwen, what is this swill?"

"The supplier brought us bad wine last week. This is why he's been fired. I've just finished speaking to you about it. Besides, it's not that bad."

"Whatever this is, it's terrible!"

"Hence why he no longer brings our goods. What you have there is whisky. A newer batch. The older, and better tasting has already been sold to pay for more livestock." She took a bite of a cooked carrot. "Really, does no one *ever* listen to me?"

Flora groaned and drained her cup, then Gwen's, then called for another. Usually her sister would by trying to pry the glass from her fingers, but that night, she stayed silent. Flora welcomed the relief the alcohol gave her and briefly thought that, maybe in her spinster years, she'd own a winery. Or perhaps move to America and make rum. She could pass her loveless years in a drunken stupor, living in the woods among all the wildlife.

"Yes, just me and all the American bears and beavers and…rum…" she muttered over the lip of her cup.

"What?" Gwen was barely containing a laugh.

Flora felt her cheeks pink. "Nothing."

"Are you drunk yet?"

"Well, the floor is spinning and I want to sleep, so I think that's what it means."

"Good," Gwen said shortly before rising from her chair.

"Everything all right?" Penelope asked from farther down the table as she placed a squirming Ian on the floor.

Flora nodded as she stood. "I'm just very tired from traveling."

"Verra drunk, from the look o' it." Drum laughed.

"Leave her be," Gwen ordered, stepping off the platform and gliding down the path through the tables. She took quite the place of the little mother when Charlotte was gone. "Come along, Flora."

"Can I come along too?" Ian asked hopefully, looking up at Flora.

"Of course you can." Flora held out her hand for him to take and they scurried from the room, following Gwen's graceful stride.

"Where are we goin'?" Ian questioned, excited to be on a nocturnal adventure.

"Just to my chamber," Flora explained. "I had a very long train ride and I'm very tired."

Ian huffed. "Oh, I thought we'd be doin'

somethin' fun."

"A sleepover can be fun. Would you like to have a sleepover?"

He grinned. "Aye, I would! What is it?"

"Well, remember when you first came to live with us and you would sleep with Charlotte until you got your own room?"

"Aye," he answered as they began climbing the stairs.

"It's like that. You can sleep in my room tonight, and in the morning, maybe we'll have breakfast in bed."

"Nanny never lets me eat in bed."

"Well, I don't have a nanny anymore and I make my own rules," Flora told him. Having him around was instantly lifting her mood. His young enthusiasm made her feel wistful of her own innocence.

"Will you two hurry up?" Gwen groaned from Flora's bedroom door as they came to the landing.

Ian released Flora's hand and scrambled down the hall to Gwen. "Miss Gwendolyn, may I have some hot chocolate?"

"Miss Gwendolyn?" Flora mimicked. "My, how proper."

"He's only like that when he wants something," Gwen clarified as she opened the door for Ian.

"I have manners!" he bellowed, climbing atop Flora's bed and beginning to jump, causing several decorative pillows to tumble to the floor.

Flora giggled and sat before the fire. The alcohol and Ian had loosened her greatly. "Gwen, ring for a maid. I think we could all do with a treat."

***

When the cakes and chocolates were eaten, and Ian was curled up asleep in Flora's bed, she began to feel at home at last. With her closest sister by her side, she could pretend that everything was normal, completely ordinary. Although her subconscious still picked painfully at thoughts, filling them with regret and annoying whispers of *what if*...and the voices only got louder with every passing moment of silence.

Flora looked at Gwen, who was polishing off the last of the tarts. She was so at ease, comfortable, and horridly quiet. Gwen hummed a bit to herself and twirled a curl around her finger as if she hadn't a care in the world. It was as if she gave no thought to her elder sister's suffering. The cow.

"Aren't you going to say something?" Flora snapped.

Gwen's fair brows rose in surprise. "Excuse me?"

"You're excused." She crossed her arms and slumped deeper into her armchair. "Now, aren't you going to pester me? Ask me a hundred questions?"

"Why would I?" She sounded honestly befuddled. "You begged me not to, and I haven't."

Flora bit her lip and slumped a bit in her chair. She *had* forbidden Gwen from speaking of Andrew. "Oh, I'd forgotten."

"If you'd like to tell me what happened, I'll listen."

"I think I should."

Gwen nodded in agreement.

161

Flora took a deep breath, letting the air fill her lungs, then exit slowly. "Well, you obviously know everything that happened until I left for London, so I'll start from there. Charlie and I ran into Andrew as soon—"

"Andrew?"

"Andrew Philips. He's friends with—"

Gwen help up her hand. "Wait, yes, I remember him. Tall, red-haired, odd speech."

"His speech is fine. As I was saying, we were in the carriage when—"

"So he no longer has a stutter?"

Flora groaned in annoyance. "Gwendolyn, if you don't stop interrupting me, I'll never finish this story. Just let me speak."

Gwen pursed her lips dramatically and nodded for Flora to continue.

"After Charlie and I ran into Andrew, Andrew started to come round fairly often. We had tea, went to an opera, and he invited me to his uncle's ball. He…he told me that he…*cared* for me."

"That sounds lovely."

Flora ran her finger along the top of her china cup. "It was…until it wasn't. Until I told him I couldn't accept his adoration and left him in the snow, calling out to me to listen."

"Do you dislike him then?"

"No, there was nothing to dislike."

"I see," she murmured softly. "And then you decided to leave him?"

"Well, when you say it so plainly, yes. That's exactly what happened."

"Why?"

"Everyone keeps asking that." Flora hung her head low, practically placing it in her lap.

Gwen snatched the top of her hair and yanked her upward as she used to do when they were children, then leaned back in her seat. "You can't hide from me."

"Ouch! Gwen, you're being a perfect monster."

"I believe the young man you abandoned could say the same about you," Gwen retorted with a scowl. "What in the world happened to make you dislike him so?"

"He's a pure gentleman. After what happened with Jasper, I could never agree to allow him to grow closer to me."

Gwen's sapphire eyes widened. "Mercy, Flora, I'd completely forgotten...you're not...*with child*?"

"No, thank goodness."

"Then what's the matter?"

"Don't make me spell it out."

"Flora, I promise you that I will not mention Andrew again after this day. But you're so much like when Drum returned without Penelope. Imagine who he would have been if not for her, and really think about whether you're ready to leave Andrew forever."

"I've already left and it's done," she said, gazing into the dying embers of the fire.

"Then I will never speak of him again."

When Gwen promised to leave all mention of Andrew behind, Flora believed her. Gwen was always kind, in that way. She knew when to meddle and when to steer clear of a topic. Flora was grateful for her, as she lay curled around Ian's little body once Gwen had gone to her own room to sleep.

Flora tried to focus on the little boy as they laid together in the dark. His small, five-year-old fingers gripped hers tightly and he kicked a bit in his sleep. She suppressed a laugh and pulled him closer, breathing in his little boy scent of milk and soap. In the summers he would be hot, sweaty, and smelling like grass and wet dog.

She wondered if she'd even hold her own child like she held Ian. Flora had never thought far enough ahead for babies, only about settling down into marriage. But much of her time in London was spent worrying if she was in the family way and then, having Ian by her side again, it made her think how she would feel to have her own.

On a whim, she quietly knocked twice on the wall above her headboard as she had done so many times in her life that the striped paper above her bed was slightly worn. Gwen crept in almost at once and slipped beneath the covers on the other side of Ian. Gwen took Flora's free hand and squeezed her fingers tightly.

Flora bit back the flood of painful sobs that burned the back of her throat. She and Gwen had always had a special bond. They were not twins; there was more than a year between them. But they shared a connection and could feel each other's emotions. She hoped Gwen wasn't feeling her pain at that moment. She hoped her little sister would never feel the thrashing defeat that buried itself deep in her chest, burning her lungs with every stifled breath.

They lay together in the dark, listening to the waves crash along the cliffs below. Gwen held Flora's hand as she wept the bitter tears of loss. And good to her word, Gwen stayed silent.

Chapter Thirteen

Flora had just finished her tea when she heard the sound of horses galloping toward the castle. She assumed it was just the usual messengers who came and went from the keep like clockwork, especially so close to tax season and Martinmas. So she strolled through the halls toward Conner's study, where she planned to steal a few of his newer novels to bide her day.

She curled up in an armchair, tucked away in an alcove, with a book featuring a wealthy princess and a handsome pirate king. The pair had just boarded the ship for the first time when the door crashed open with a bang. She glanced toward the noise and her eyes were instantly drawn to a toothy grin and a mane of wild orange hair.

"Charlie?" she squawked, dropping her book to the floor and losing her place.

"Obviously." He strolled toward her, pausing at Conner's desk to inspect a pickled specimen.

Flora was too stunned by his sudden appearance to move. "What are you doing here?"

166

"When I heard you ran back to Scotland, I said to myself, 'Charlie, you dashing devil, trouble follows Flora wherever she goes and what better trouble is there in this world than you, Charles, Duke of Fenton?'"

"So you immediately got on a train to follow me?"

"What else was a man to do?"

"Stay home in London and take care of your responsibilities?"

He chuckled. "While you immerse yourself in a sea of kilts, leaving none for me? Hardly!"

"I'm not immersing myself in anything, presently," she grumbled. "But I am happy to see you."

"Who wouldn't be?" He came to her chair and gave her a pat upon the head. "And I've even brought you a gift."

The corners of her lips rose. "A gift?"

"Oh, yes. A wonderful surprise."

Flora felt her heart lift. Charlie was always a fantastic gift giver, mainly thanks to his interest in flying through his family's unlimited funds with the wild abandon of a true blueblood. "What is it?"

He produced a strand of thick ribbon from his coat pocket. "Put this on and I'll take you to it."

Flora leaped up and allowed him to place the covering over her eyes. "Charlie, this is exactly what I needed right now."

"Oh, I know," he replied as he took one of her hands and began leading her.

She tried picturing where they were in the castle as they walked. But after several strange turns,

Flora couldn't imagine where they could be. She even thought Charlie might have been dragging her in circles. After the eighth set of stairs, Flora was flushed, sweaty, and completely annoyed.

"How is it that we've gone up and down eight stairways when the castle is only four levels?"

"I got lost," he told her, his voice wavering through bouts of stifled giggles.

Flora pulled her hand from Charlie's grip. "I'm not moving another inch until you stop this nonsense."

"I'm sorry, Flora, just a few more steps. I promise that I'm finished taking the scenic route."

"Fine." She allowed Charlie to lead her for a few moments more before he stopped her. "Finally. Can I take this blindfold off now?" When he didn't respond, she called out, "Charlie?"

A set of hands untied the ribbon, and Flora blinked several times as she tried to acclimate herself to the bright light. She was about to chastise Charlie for his theatrics when she found herself looking not at the joking duke, but at Andrew Philips.

"Surprise!" Charlie cheered from off to the side, throwing his long arms in the air.

Flora felt ill. The walls were closing in on her and she thought she might be sick. "Andrew?" she croaked.

"Flora." He nodded.

"Well, this is no fun," Charlie grumbled, sulking.

She whipped toward him. "Is this nothing but a lark to you?"

He huffed. "Of course not. I was just expecting a

bit more positivity all around."

"I'm sorry, Flora," Andrew cut in. "I thought…Charlie told me that you would be pleased."

She turned back to Andrew, but she couldn't raise her eyes to look at his face. Instead, she stared at the floor. "It's not that I'm displeased…it's just…I'm…"

"*Surprised*?" Charlie sang, his tone hopeful.

"Do be quiet, Charles," Andrew barked in a harsh, deep voice that sounded very much unlike his own. Then his tone softened. "Flora, I'm terribly sorry this happened. Upsetting you wasn't my intention at all."

"I know," she responded with a small sniff. She was on the verge of tears, and not the delicate droplets that made a woman's eyes glow like when Penelope wept, but ugly sobs that would blotch her face.

Flora dared a glance at Andrew, who was staring at her openly. His face was almost unreadable. But his eyes had dark circles beneath them and there was a dusting of scruff on his jaw that she had never seen before. It looked as if he hadn't slept in days.

Charlie whistled, breaking the spell. "Well! What's there to eat? I'm famished."

"Do be *quiet*, Charles!" Andrew snapped.

"What's this, then?" Drum had appeared in the doorway. He was fastening his sword around his waist.

Andrew nodded to him. "Mr. MacGregor, how do you do?"

Drum looked startled. He glanced at Flora, who

shrugged in response. "Andrew Philips? What brings ye to Scotland?"

"Andy and I fancied some fresh air," Charlie said.

"Then fancy a ride with me, Charlie?" Drum grinned. "Much more fresh air to be had out in the hills."

Charlie scoffed. "Goodness, no. It's much too cold. My hands will get chapped."

"Will you both stay in the castle?" Gwen stood in the doorway of the sitting room.

Flora felt the parlor was becoming exceedingly crowded, but she still said, "Yes, we have plenty of room."

"If it will be of no imposition?" Andrew's eyes were trained on her.

"Not at all!" Gwen exclaimed. "I'll have the footmen bring up your things. Flora, why don't you show our guests to the green and red rooms?"

Flora nodded wordlessly, beckoning both to follow her. She led the way up both flights of stairs to the third floor, conscious of each and every one of Andrew's footsteps behind her. When they got to the landing, she steered them right, where the nicer guest rooms were situated. To the left were smaller ones where Conner's men, who didn't fit above the stable, stayed.

Charlie immediately shouted, "I call the red room!" And he disappeared behind its door.

"Then I suppose the green is yours." Flora motioned to the closed door. "If you need anything, there will be a pull next to the bed, which will summon the help."

"It's the same room I had when I came for Penelope's wedding."

"Oh."

"Flora, I—"

"Your bag, Mr. Philips," a stocky footman interrupted.

Andrew tore his gaze from Flora. "Ah, yes, thank you."

"We will be having supper within the hour," she told him, eager to flee, but not wanting to appear rude.

"Flora...could I have a moment of your time?"

"I...I must go ready myself for dinner."

He nodded. "Yes, yes, you're right."

"I'll see downstairs," she mumbled, then scurried through the hallway, down the stairs, and into her bedroom, barely missing a startled Gwen.

Flora begged her sister to leave it be and audibly groaned when Gwen entered, closing the door behind her. She waited for Gwen make some sort of remark, and found it odd when she merely crossed to the wardrobe and asked, "May I borrow your pink slippers?"

"Slippers?" Flora mimicked. "*Slippers*? Aren't you going to mention Andrew *at all*?"

"No." Her voice was pleasant, nonchalant, and void of any curiosity.

Flora remembered Gwen's promise to never speak of Andrew again. She could kick herself for allowing it again. "I know you told me that Andrew would never come up, but he's here, in our home, and I need you to forgo your promise and help me."

Gwen's shoulders relaxed and she turned from

the dresser with a smile. "Thank goodness. I can't even fit into your shoes! Your feet are gigantic."

"What do I do?"

"I don't see why you're asking me. I barely know the man! What do you *want* to do? And I mean honestly, without any thought."

"I want to…I…" Flora faltered. She had thought of little else besides what she wished could be, but putting her feelings into words was much more difficult than she thought. "If I was a different person, I would allow Andrew to know me. I would go with him to the opera, and stay the whole duration. I would go with him to tea and the Stoneward Hotel and accompany him to dinner. I would do all the things that anyone else would."

"But you're not someone else," Gwen pointed out. "You're Flora, and that's enough."

Flora felt her eyes well and took a deep breath to bid them back. The last thing she needed was to be blotchy and swollen when she went downstairs for dinner. "I…I just…I need to dress."

"And you'll wear your cream velvet gown and your seed pearls with your hair long."

She patted the bun atop her head. She had rather taken to the English way of dress. And Andrew, as an English man, may think that a woman with her hair long was immoral. And so when she opened the doors of her wardrobe to get her dress, she whispered, "I think I might leave it up."

***

Andrew, Charlie, Drum, and Penelope were all

172

in the drawing room when Gwen and Flora came down for supper. She skimmed the edge of the room to where Penelope sat, far away from Andrew.

"Hello, feeling better?" Penelope was resplendent in a peach gown and smiled up at Flora before lowering her voice. "Did you invite Charlie and Andrew?"

"Did Drum tell you everything?" Flora felt her stomach knot.

"How am I to know? All he said was that you and Andrew were somehow involved and had a falling out, of sorts. You needn't tell me any more than that. And if his presence makes you uncomfortable, we'll have him leave."

"No, don't." She shot her gaze toward Andrew, who was watching her intently. "Just…act normal."

"I am. *You're* the one who's laced too tight."

"Am not."

Penelope grabbed Flora's arm and pulled her down on the chaise beside her. "You look like frightened deer. Your eyes are wide and you appear as if you might faint at any time."

"Because I might."

"Flora, how can I help you?"

She shrugged. "How could I know? I can barely help myself."

"You're so terribly…*Scottish*."

Flora let out a short, startled laugh. "Is that so?"

Penelope nodded. "Yes, you're all silent stones until you crack under the pressure of your own weight."

"Who's a stone then, lass?" Drum questioned as he approached them.

"No one," Penelope answered, allowing Drum to help her up. "Is dinner ready?"

"Aye, in the dinin' room," he responded, kissing his wife on the top of her head.

"Why not the feasting hall?" Flora asked. "We hardly ever eat supper in the dining room."

"The maids are havin' it all primed and polished to prepare for Martinmas," Drum explained as he turned to take Penelope to dine. "Conner said he'd be back by then."

"May I escort you, my lady?" Charlie came to Flora and bowed dramatically at the waist.

Flora rolled her eyes, but took his arm and whispered, "Thank you. I certainly thought you would have forced me to sit with Andrew."

"You don't want to?"

"I want you to stop prying, that's what I want."

"But I can't!" he yelped, clutching his heart. "I'd *die*!"

From the corner of her vision, she saw Gwen take Andrew's arm. Although she knew she had no right, a pang of irrational jealousy lurched within her breast at seeing her sister so near to him.

"Well, someone's a bit envious of their younger sister," Charlie sang.

"Do you ever stop?"

"No, it's a curse and a gift, my darling." He looked around the table as everyone else sat and then the corners of his long mouth rose.

Flora recognized his devious stare. "Don't. You. Dare."

"Andy, old boy!" Charlie bellowed. "We really must switch seats. You see, I'm facing the window, which I cannot possibly do past sundown."

"What in the world is he talkin' about?" Drum murmured, slack jawed.

"Tis true, my large, plaid friend," Charlie affirmed. "Seeing the trees in the dark is bad for my digestion. It's much better for me to sit facing the fireplace. You understand, Andy, don't you?"

"Certainly," Andrew responded in a dry voice that hinted he knew Charlie was goading them on. Still, he rose from his place and exchanged with Charlie, presumably to stop him from partaking in any more dramatics.

Flora tried locking eyes with Charlie, but the cad kept his attention on everything other than the enraged woman on the other side of the table. She swore she would get her revenge, but focused instead on her meal. She counted each piece of fish she cut, every potato the footman put on her plate. She pondered every ingredient in the soup, and pushed away the proffered wine, unable to take a chance of getting drunk and making her tongue loose. And although the cook had served creampuffs for dessert, she couldn't stomach a single bite.

Andrew was so close, she could smell his faint cologne. When they were in the sitting room, she noticed he'd shaved his face and brushed his thick hair back from his forehead. He looked just like he had the night of his uncle's party when he had asked to become better, more intimately, acquainted. Andrew's hand sat upon the table, and Flora fought the irrational urge to take it in her own.

"Yes, *Flora*, do show dear Andy the study!"

Charlie exclaimed as he finished his fourth glass. "I'm sure there's a specimen or two that will *titillate* you both."

"What's that, now?" Drum glared at Charlie.

Penelope slapped Charlie on the arm with her folded fan. "Behave."

"What's in the study?" Andrew asked, speaking for the first time since he'd moved to sit beside Flora.

"Conner likes to collect things," Gwen said. "Mostly books, but sometimes pickled animals and exotic things the traders bring."

"Would he mind me looking at his collection?" Andrew asked eagerly, the ghost of a smile touching his lips.

Drum shook his head and yawned. "No, no' at all."

Andrew turned to her. "Flora, could you show me the study?"

Flora felt the blood rush from her face, but everyone attending the dinner party was watching her. "Of course. Whenever you're finished, we'll go."

"Oh, I'm finished."

"Marvelous." She picked up her previously untouched glass and emptied it in one large, unladylike swallow. "Follow me."

"I say!" she heard Charlie exclaim as she rose from her seat and walked from the room.

Andrew followed and caught up to her as soon as they were in the flame-lit corridor.

"It's only right this way," she murmured, her gaze on the floor as she walked. Flora waited for

176

Andrew to speak, to try to pry from her the reasons for her leaving, but he merely strolled beside her, silent and observant.

The large doors to Conner's private library and study squeaked as she pushed them open. The only light in the room came from the single, large fireplace. She went to the desk and lit an oil lamp. Andrew took it and walked the edge of the room, peering into shelves and studying things in small jars. She stood by the fire and waited for him to finish, but he got to the stairs to the library's second floor first.

"Where do these go?"

"Up to a second section of older books and then to the top of the keep."

"Fascinating architecture."

Flora was puzzled by his calm study of the room, but still followed him as he climbed the spiral staircase. She watched as he bent to inspect the titles of several books, and then trailed him again as he went back down to main floor and set the lamp upon Conner's desk.

After several tense moments of silence, Andrew opened his mouth. "Flora, I know you didn't ask me to come. I know me being here isn't what you would have chosen. But I couldn't live with myself if I didn't try...if I didn't truly try to show you that I can be the man you need."

Flora wanted to run, but her feet were planted firmly on the floor, rooted to the stone beneath them. She couldn't even bring herself to speak. Andrew grew near, each step light. It was as if he knew she wanted to dash off and evade capture, so he was slowly moving closer, as if he hoped to catch her before she disappeared.

"Please, Flora." He reached up and brushed his fingers over the curve of her shoulder, drew it down her arm, then took her hand in his.

His grip was strong and sure. She stared down at their link, afraid to look anywhere else. "Andrew, you don't understand."

"Make me understand, Flora. And if you don't care for me…if you can't stand the sight of me, then I'll leave now and you'll never see me again in Scotland, or London if I can help it."

"It's not that I don't care for you. I…I just can't let you…" She was humiliated to feel the sharp pricks of hot tears begin to well. "I wish things were simple."

He cupped her cheek with a hand, pulling her gaze to meet his. "Flora, nothing in life is simple. But my feelings for you are. Just tell me what's stopping you."

"I can't." Her voice was small, but she felt even tinier than she sounded. "I can't tell you."

"Why not?"

"You'll hate me and think I'm terrible."

Andrew brushed away a stray tear with his thumb. "Have you killed anyone?"

"No."

"Have you stolen something valuable or irreplaceable from me?"

"No, of course not," she replied, confused as to the relevance of his questioning.

"Have you done anything to intentionally cause me harm?"

Flora's lips trembled. "I would never."

"Then nothing you could tell me would make me hate you."

She decided it was then, or never. Once she told him who she really was—what she did—he would leave, and this cruel game of promised love would finally end. Flora felt she could try to move on with her life if she knew Andrew despised her.

"Before I came to London, I...I did things that I'm ashamed of," Flora confessed through her tears. "Things that I don't wish to speak of."

"Flora..." Andrew whispered, the sound of her name barely louder than the crackling of the fireplace.

She turned her face away. "Please, don't ask me to say anything more."

"I don't need to know anything more. I don't care about your past, your secrets, or your flaws. I only think of you now, as you are in this moment, so beautiful and complex in a way that makes you perfect to me."

Andrew released her hand and wrapped his arms around her. His palm circled her back and she could hear the steady thump of his heart and feel his chest move with every breath. Flora felt as if she could stay locked within that moment forever, no matter how selfish it was of him.

"Flora?"

"Yes?"

"If you care for me, even the smallest bit, then let me stay," he implored her.

Flora pondered his request. She hated the thought of him wasting his time with her, but Drum and Gwen were right. He was man who had to make his own decisions, even if they weren't the right ones. She decided to allow him to live his own life, but wouldn't lead him to believe that she would be a healthy part of it. He needed to see her, as she was, as Scottish as she was, as flawed as she was. Only then would he be free.

"You can stay."

Chapter Fourteen

"I'd really rather not," Flora said to Gwen as they were cloistered in her bedchambers the next morning.

"You need to participate as a sister of the laird. There's no other way."

Flora held up her hands, slender and white. "Do you see these fingers, Gwen? They were not meant to participate in the slaughter of cows!"

"I've told you that we are shorthanded. We'll be able to hire more staff when the villagers all come up for the Martinmas celebrations, but until then, we're quite on our own." Gwen sighed as she buttoned up the back of Flora's simple green day dress. "Besides, you're not actually going to be doing any of the slaughtering."

"I don't want to touch the blood," Flora complained, thinking of the disgusting way the cook and her helpers mashed the blood and oatmeal mixture with their hands before putting it into the casing. It was enough to make her ill.

Gwen stepped back and grabbed Flora's arm,

turning her around to face her. "You can either cook in the kitchen or clean the guest rooms with the maids. I'm not saying you need to scrub the stones, but you *will* be at work for the next two days until Martinmas."

"And what will *you* be doing while I'm working my elegant fingers to the bone?"

She averted her eyes in a rather guilty manner before squaring her shoulders and saying, "I will be keeping a detailed account of all the goings on in the keep."

"So, nothing?"

Gwen's rounded cheeks flamed red, but her expression was short-lived. "It is not nothing. We need to know the numbers of animals slaughtered, the casks of ale and wine opened, the taxes that are brought...it's very detail oriented work." She balled her little hands upon her hips and scowled. "And if you think you can handle the numbers better than I, then by all means have at it!"

Flora held up her hands. "I surrender. I'll try to help where I can."

Her younger sister nodded, seemingly mollified. "Good. Then hurry along." She made a move to leave, but stopped. "Wait, perhaps you could be of help to Penelope?"

"Oh, yes! What is she doing?" Flora knew that whatever Penelope was assigned, it would certainly be nothing too dirty or strenuous. Drum just wouldn't allow it.

As soon as Gwen was gone, and Flora had wrapped herself in a thick brown cloak lined with fur, she went downstairs to find Penelope. Shouts could be heard emanating from outside. She followed the din out into the courtyard.

To her right, a small group of men were practicing archery. To her left, piles of wood were being assembled for bonfires. The long wooden tables from the feasting hall were also being dragged out for the nights of non-stop revelry that would take place.

She spied Penelope standing near the open gate, seemingly waiting for something.

Flora went to her and tapped her on the shoulder before asking, "What are you doing?"

Penelope jumped slightly. "Goodness, Flora, you startled me. And everything is fine, I'm just waiting for the wagons to arrive."

"What wagons?"

She shrugged. "Apparently the casks of ale are late and I'm to yell at them once they arrive."

"Ooh, can I help?"

"I don't know. Did Gwen give you something to do?"

"Help you? I don't remember, honestly. I just know that I don't wish to be in the kitchens."

Penelope laughed. "And I don't blame you. Gwen told me how many vats of blood they were sieving down there." She shivered dramatically.

"So I take it me standing here with you would be helpful?" Flora asked hopefully. She prayed Penelope would allow her to stand guard with her, but it was not to be.

"Sadly, Gwen would be quite vexed with us if you were to be here idle and it doesn't take two to yell at a man."

Flora sighed and peered around the courtyard. "Surely there must be something I can do that doesn't require me to be up to my elbows in blood."

"Why don't you go find Charlie?" she suggested as a wagon piled high with barrels came into view. "Drum's given him some sort of job, but knowing Charlie he's found a nice hiding place. Perhaps you could join him?"

"Splendid idea!" Flora turned and went in search of her favorite rabble-rouser.

It didn't take long; she could hear his voice ringing out, clear as a highly pitched bell. The noise echoed off the stone walls of the keep and Flora followed it until she spied him near the armory, where a dozen men were sparring with swords.

"Flora, you darling creature!" Charlie greeted her with a kiss upon the cheek then gestured broadly to the men before him. "Isn't it a fine morning for such entertainment?"

"Hmm, yes," she muttered, uninterested in watching the Scotsmen she had known all her life. "What job has Gwen given you?"

"Andy and I were meant to take account of the weapons. Or arrows?" He shook his head. "Some such thing."

"Andrew?" Flora glanced around the yard, but he was nowhere to be seen.

Charlie, seemingly noticing her unease, told her, "Don't fret. I believe he's in that sword shed thing, actually doing what we were told."

Just then, Andrew appeared from within the armory, a sheet of paper full of numbers clutched in his hand. He skimmed the sheet again then looked at each swordsman in turn before nodding to himself and tucking the paper into the breast pocket of his jacket.

"Andy, you old so-and-so," Charlie crooned. "Get our work done and stop dawdling, will you?"

"Aye, *Andy*," an older warrior named Douglas sang out to him. "Did ye count the tools *real* men use, laddie?"

The rest of the Scotsmen laughed along with Douglas and Flora felt her cheeks grow hot. They were poking fun at him for doing something his sister had ordered. She was about to give Douglas a piece of her mind, but Charlie got there first.

"Now see here…whatever your name is, Andy is quite the accomplished fencer and you'd do well to keep that in mind!"

Douglas burst out into chuckles and turned to his friends, saying something in Scottish that Flora had good sense to not repeat. Andrew, on the other hand, merely nodded in their direction and continued on his way. He passed Charlie and Flora with a simple, "Good day."

Once Andrew had rounded the corner and was firmly out of sight, Douglas and the rest continued their spar, making Gaelic remarks about the softness of British men. Flora felt another hot flash of fury at their jokes and crossed her arms over her chest to quell the rapid anger-fueled pounding of her heart. She saw Charlie watching her with a ridiculous grin on his freckled face.

"My, aren't we testy?" he asked as Flora turned from him and began to walk away from the armory.

"No, I'm fine."

"Darling Flora, your face is as red as my hair."

She brought a hand to her cheek. "It's just the cold."

"It is rather frozen this far north, isn't it?"

"Scotland's a cold, wet country."

Charlie stopped. "Oh, no."

"What is it?" she asked, but then followed his stare. Gwen was stalking toward them.

"Hide!" Charlie turned on his heel and dashed away, leaving Flora on her own.

"What are you doing?" Gwen asked in a harsh voice that didn't seem to match her golden cherub looks.

"I was helping Charlie—"

"Helping Charlie avoid his work? Yes, I'm aware."

Flora looked around guiltily. "Penelope didn't need any assistance."

"At which point you should have come back to me." She thrust something toward Flora, who took it without thinking.

"Now, get down to the kitchens and make yourself useful!" Gwen stalked off, presumably to order someone else about.

When Flora unraveled the ball of gray fabric, she saw that Gwen had given her an apron. Muttering to herself, and cursing her little sister, she resigned herself to the kitchens and said goodbye to her beautiful hands.

***

By the time the black pudding was made, the

sausages cased, and the bloody mess in the kitchen mostly clean, Flora was ready to fall into bed. She wondered how the poor kitchen maids worked so hard day in and day out. While she had always fancied herself a strong woman, she was clearly mistaken.

Her afternoon in the kitchen had stained her frock, mussed her hair, and made Flora smell like the metallic scent of blood and meat. She couldn't wait to rid herself of her ruined clothes and soak in a fragrant bath to wash away the disgusting layer of sweat and animal filth that coated her. Dinner would be served in two short hours, so she had to hurry.

Flora was about to turn to the stairs that led up to her chambers when she crashed into something firm. Startled, she looked up, coming face to face with Andrew. "Goodness, I'm sorry, I wasn't watching where I was going."

"No harm done." His brown eyes grazed Flora, sending a rush of heat through her body.

He was used to the fine ladies of London in their silk gowns and impeccably coiled locks. And there she was, mussed, matted, and stained with animal blood. "I'm sorry you have to see me like this. I was just on my way to change."

A small smile touched Andrew's lips and he reached up to tuck a loose strand of her hair behind her ear. "You look lovely, Flora."

"Don't tease me," she ordered, her gaze falling to the floor. She felt so humiliated at being seen in such a state. She had made a reputation of being poised and delicate, not smeared with red. "I know what I look like."

"Obviously you don't." He gently touched her chin, raising her face upward, forcing their gazes to meet. "I've seen you dressed for a ball and dressed for the kitchens. Each version is perfection."

Flora swallowed the urge to run, not that her tired legs would participate. She thought she should say something, but all her words stuck in her dry throat. She was never prepared for Andrew, nor the confusing swirl of emotions he caused to fly through her chest—hope, fear, adoration, bewilderment…lust.

"I'll let you get ready for dinner. Will you sit beside me?" he asked, his hand still cupped along her jaw.

She nodded, still unable to speak.

Andrew nodded slightly, then pressed his lips carefully, softly upon her forehead for just a moment before releasing her, leaving on his way, wherever he was going. Flora leaned back against the wall for support, feeling as if her legs wouldn't hold her weight any longer.

"Dear Lord," she rasped. "I'm not even wearing a corset and I still can't bloody breathe."

"Language!" a voice chastised from the top of the stairs.

Flora jumped and looked up, seeing Gwen sitting on the steps. "How long were you there?"

"Long enough."

She righted herself and balled her gown in her hands as she strode up the stairs, hoping the inevitable flush was gone from her cheeks. But judging by Gwen's lifted eyebrows and bemused expression, she was sure it was not.

"I'm going to go wash the kitchen stench off," Flora announced as she passed.

"Lovely," Gwen said, rising and following Flora. "I'll come keep you company."

"I don't *need* company," she spat, a bit harsher than she meant.

Gwen stopped Flora from shutting the door in her face. "But I have something I know you like. Something that will make your bath all the more pleasant."

Flora paused. Gwen knew exactly how to force her hand. "What is it?"

She held up a small glass bottle, showing off a green-tinted oil. "Eucalyptus."

"Dash it all, Gwen. You know I can't deny you when you have my favorite scent." She opened her door wide to allow her entry.

"I ordered it specially through the Portuguese ship. I wasn't sure if they had gotten my order, as it was sent not many weeks ago," she explained as Flora took the vial and began filling her bath.

"Well, thank you for thinking of me."

"Of course. I'll even let you bathe in peace."

"Aren't you in a giving mood?"

"But I would like to make one small request, if I may?"

Flora's stomach lurched. "If you must."

"Andrew is a good man. I don't know him well, but I know enough to see that he cares for you deeply. If you don't love him, send him home, and end his misery."

She couldn't answer with words. So she merely

nodded and waited until Gwen had left before lowering herself into the water. As much as she hated to admit it, Gwen was right. It wouldn't be fair of her to string Andrew along. But if she did care, *did* love him like she felt she may, then maybe she would allow him to stay, if only for her own selfish desire to see him.

"Yes," she whispered to herself, knowing that no one would hear her. "Maybe I do love him."

***

Flora took extra care in dressing before going down for supper. She had her maid pin her hair as it would have been in England and put on a pale green gown with white piping. She hoped she would look as British as possible, as strange as that sounded. Andrew spent his life in the company of carefully poised English roses like Penelope and Flora would hate to appear coarse and rustic.

Before she left for dinner, she grabbed an ivory fan and practiced the graceful way Penelope walked; it was like a ship, gliding over a smooth sea. Andrew would like a woman who walked confidently like that. No, he *deserved* a woman like that, who would fit in seamlessly with the other barristers and their fine, English wives.

When Flora came to the sitting room, she smiled inwardly when she saw Andrew's gaze roll over her appreciatively. She waited for him to approach her, which he did within moments of her entering.

"You look lovely," he murmured.

"Thank you." She opened up her fan and

fluttered it before her face in a way she hoped was coy.

"Are you excited for the festivities tomorrow?" Andrew asked as he escorted her to the dining table.

"Yes, Martinmas is always a lot of fun. People travel from all over the highlands."

After he helped her into a seat, he took his own. "And what does one do as a Martinmas celebration?"

"Well, the tenants pay their taxes and everyone begins the winter preparations. Usually the excess animals are slaughtered and the harvests are all taken in."

"Is that why there was...blood in your hair?" he questioned quietly and in a very serious manner.

Flora frowned and turned to her meal, embarrassed at being reminded of her earlier state. "Yes," she mumbled. "It was for the black pudding."

"Then I'm sure it'll be delicious," Andrew murmured, his face close to hers.

She felt flattered and was trying to think of something witty to say when Charlie caught her eye. He was all teeth as he stared at the pair in obvious, unabashed enjoyment. Flora bobbed her head slightly to her left, hiding behind an artful display of harvest wheat that sat as a display upon the table.

"Did you hear that?" Gwen asked from her right.

"What?" Flora hadn't been listening to anything anyone was saying.

"Drum said that when Conner comes home, there will be a horse race!" Gwen was flushed. She adored horse races and didn't miss a single one when they ran near the castle. Flora suspected her quiet sister might even make a bet or two, but never asked, as Conner would certainly never approve of gambling.

"That's rather exciting." Andrew leaned toward them. "I was in the stables earlier and I must say that you have such marvelous beasts."

"Will you participate, Mr. Philips?" Gwen asked.

Andrew chuckled a bit, but didn't seem all that amused. "As tempting as that may be, I admit that I'm not an overly accomplished horseman. Especially when it comes to Clydesdales."

"Will ye spar, then?" Drum called from the other end of the table. "Or join in with the archery? There's always a fair prize for the caber toss as well."

"Oh, yes," Gwen said. "You know, Drum took first place the year before last."

Drum grinned and looked at his wife. "Aye, took on a bag o' silver for my talents. But no need for that, this year. Our farm does quite well. Although I may compete all the same."

"But dear old Andy is a superb fencer, aren't you, Andy?" Charlie had pushed the centerpiece aside.

Andrew shrugged and put down his fork. "I wouldn't go that far."

"Look, he's being modest," Charlie crooned. "Go on Andy, tell us all about your fancy fencing tutors at Eaton."

Noticing Andrew's growing unease, Flora commanded, "Stop teasing Andrew, Charlie, and tell us what *you* will be participating in."

Charlie didn't miss a beat. "Will there be a kissing booth? I was at a fair this summer where you paid—"

"No," Drum retorted shortly. Then he picked up a decanter of whisky and handed it to Charlie. "Have at this, then."

Charlie grinned. "Don't mind if I do."

"Pay him no mind," Flora told Andrew under her breath. "He just wants to goad you into a fight."

Andrew didn't seem at all flustered by Charlie's behavior. "Perhaps I will join in on a competition or two in the spirit of things."

"Just stay away from the archery, aye?" Drum warned good-naturedly. "I may be a fine thrower, but I'm the best archer in the highlands."

As the conversation tore away from the games into an account of the estate by Gwen, Flora studied. And by studied, she watched Penelope's every move. She examined her hands as Penelope took small bites of her food and delicate sips of cider. Flora even took note of the way Penelope flirted with Drum—a light hand upon his arm as they spoke and a playful bat of her lashes when he looked her way.

Penelope made being a lady look so effortless. But Flora's back hurt from sitting up straight and she couldn't imagine how Penelope managed to always keep her face frozen at such a pleasant state. She knew her well enough to honestly say that Penelope's movements and demeanor weren't an act, but her way of being...the way of being for a true English woman of breeding. And Flora was desperate to capture it.

Chapter Fifteen

Flora bounced on the balls of her feet as she waited for Charlie outside his bedchamber. The blasted man had made her promise to go down to the Martinmas festivities together and *he* was the late one. Conner and Charlotte had already arrived home late the night before and she could hear the sounds of villagers approaching, the din wafting through the halls—the shrill shrieks of excited children, the calls of their mothers bidding them to stay close, and the bellowing roars of the men as they shouted to one another.

She didn't mind being late, but as a MacLeod sister, she would be on display as the marriageable gem she was. And what good was being on display if no one saw her dove gray gown and white fur cloak? Certainly, she was quite focused on Andrew, but it was still nice to be acknowledged as a beauty.

"Charlie, open this door and let's go down!" She banged her fist against the door. "Hurry!"

After several quite moments, Charlie's neighbor opened their door instead. It was Andrew, presumably coming down to join the merrymaking below. He was dressed quite plainly, but elegantly, in a dark gray suit and burgundy vest. He wore no hat, and Flora was glad, as his hair shone finely in the sunlight.

"Is Charlie in trouble?" he asked as he approached.

She pointed to the closed door, a bit flustered at being caught yelling in the hall like a commoner. "He won't open the door."

His brows rose and the corners of his lips twitched. "Is that so?"

"I promised Charlie I wouldn't go downstairs without him and he refuses to come out."

"Would you like me to look in on him?"

"I tried that. He's locked the door."

Andrew pressed his cheek to the door and frowned. "Are you sure he's even in there?"

"Oh…actually, no. I just assumed he would be."

"Since he's apparently gone, might I accompany you downstairs?"

"Certainly."

The festive rousing outside hadn't spilled into the castle, not yet. The masses of people were still contained within the walls of the keep. Meat was roasting over one of the massive fires built the day before, kitchen maids milled about with jugs of ale, and a group of bagpipers played near the gate, beckoning the stragglers to come forward out of the wind and into the safety of the walls.

While the revelry was still as amusing and enthralling as always, she found her gaze drawn to Andrew. His gaze darted around the courtyard and he could barely keep still. He led her from the jugglers to the tables of sweet meats, to the pipers, and to the prized horses, all around the yard until Flora could barely catch her breath. Andrew commandeered a bench for her, and then dashed off to find her something to drink as quickly as she sat.

"Flora, where have ye been?" Conner arrived and sat beside her on the bench. "I thought I saw ye with that Philips lad."

"Because you did," Flora replied. "And I'd hardly classify him as a lad. He's almost your age."

Conner's dark blue eyes flashed. "I had heard he was here, and I wanted to see if ye needed me to oust him."

"No, I'd like him to stay."

"Really? The last I saw o' him, he was shoutin' outside in the snow as ye begged him to leave."

Flora sighed. "Well, things are different now and I'd like the chance to get to know him."

"Are ye sure, lass? Ye've been wounded by...*him*, and if this Philips lad were to harm ye, I'd have his blood on my hands and my wife would never let me hear the end o' it."

"He won't," Flora asserted firmly. "He's a gentleman of good breeding and education."

"I've seen enough learned men who appeared to be good, but ended up beatin' their wives and shirkin' their responsibilities."

"Andrew's not like them. He's kind to me, patient, and has been nothing but honest since the start and it would behoove you to respect my wishes on the matter."

He growled a bit under his breath. "I'm still

keepin' an eye on him."

"Good morning, MacLeod," Andrew greeted as he approached, a cup in his hand.

Conner nodded and watched as Andrew handed Flora the glass. "Philips."

"Thank you for the hospitality your clan has extended," Andrew began. "This Martinmas celebration is quite exciting."

"Ye know, Philips, there are many tunnels and hidden chambers within my castle."

Andrew smiled politely. "Yes, Flora has told me so much about them."

Flora averted her eyes as she felt her brother's gaze bore into her. She knew Conner would be upset at having a dramatic moment spoiled by her loud mouth, but she didn't care. She knew his game and being a bully wouldn't get him very far with Andrew.

"Well, then," Conner started slowly, after a pregnant pause. "Ye'll know that I'm always watchin', as are my men. We'll know if ye mistreat Flora, or wrong her, or go on a *midnight walk* through the halls."

Andrew didn't seem flustered by Conner's declaration and merely replied, "I would never harm Flora in any way. I hold her in the highest esteem and plan to show you that I respect her as an equal in all ways."

Conner grunted and stood, giving Andrew one last pointed look before stalking off to join the crowd.

"Goodness, he's melodramatic," Flora mumbled, feeling rather embarrassed by her brother's show of force. "I'm so sorry he interacted with you in that way."

"It doesn't bother me. But I actually met Drummond while getting your refreshment, and I must see him about something before the games begin. Do you mind?"

Flora was surprised and curious as to what Andrew needed to discuss with Drum. She hadn't known them to speak at all, if ever. She was about to ask why, but thought better than to demand answers. "Of course. Besides, I'd like to go mingle. There are many people here this year that I haven't gotten a chance to see."

He nodded in goodbye and disappeared into the crowd, leaving Flora with a cup of rapidly cooling cider. She sipped the drink slowly, watching people as they passed. She smiled in greeting at those she remembered and averted eyes when she saw Mrs. MacNee walk by with a gaggle of fire-haired children at her heels. She hoped the woman hadn't seen her, as her attention had been focused on one crying girl, but the shame she had felt hit her hard in the chest, whipping the air from her lungs.

"Oh, I'm tired!" Gwen plunked down on the bench beside her, her hair falling from her bun.

"Goodness, what's happened to you?"

She took Flora's cup from her hand and drank the rest of the cider, then put the glass down. "I've been up since sunrise preparing. I needed to ensure the taxes were all adequately filed and ready for payment. I'm so happy Conner's home to take over. He's only just relieved me from my duties."

"Yes, I just saw him. He told Andrew that he

was watching him."

"How ominous."

"It was. But he didn't scare Andrew off, which was a pleasant turn of events." Flora decided she didn't wish to discuss Andrew again, as she felt she was becoming a bit of a broken record. "What's the official line of events for the games?"

Gwen paused, biting her lip for a moment in thought before answering. "Well, if I'm not mistaken, there will be the hammer toss, then the caber toss, and archery. Tomorrow will begin with either the swordfights or the horse races, but I can't recall. Then we'll have a judging of some of the baked goods from the women in the villages."

"Quite busy."

"Yes, but it'll be good fun." Gwen stretched her neck a moment, sighing lightly. "Shall we venture out to the hammer toss? It should be starting soon."

Flora looked around to see if Andrew had returned, but he was nowhere to be seen. She felt a bit guilty at leaving their bench. What if he returned and she was gone? But she tried to brush the thoughts from her mind. He didn't exactly say he would come back for her; she merely assumed.

The games would be held outside the keep, where there was a large flat piece of land for everyone to congregate. Gwen and Flora walked over to a small platform that had been erected for the MacLeods. Conner and Charlotte were already seated, with baby Alec tucked within his mother's furs. Penelope was beside Charlotte and Charlie stood to their left, swaying a bit and with ridiculously red cheeks. Little Ian weaved between them, chasing an errant dog.

When Flora was seated between Penelope and Charlie, Charlie leaned inward. "Where's your gentleman caller, then? I thought I wouldn't be able to pry Andy from your side."

Flora shrugged. "He needed to help Drum with something, I think. I haven't seen him for some time."

"Well, well, well…" Charlie slurred, his goblet of ale to his lips. "I do believe our dear Andy has been found."

Flora followed his gaze to where the men participating in the hammer toss were approaching. She spied Drum immediately, a head taller than the rest of the men. He crossed to Penelope, holding out his hammer for her to tie her favor on. She pulled a sky blue ribbon from within her cloak and attached it quickly to the handle.

"How medieval," Charlie muttered. "Will there be jousting next?"

"It's not like that. It makes it easier to find your hammer when you throw it." She scanned the men, most of whom were going to their wives and sweethearts for their favors, then lining up, facing the empty hills beyond. "Now, where did you see Andrew?"

Charlie bobbed down slightly, so that they were eye level, and then pointed. "A shock, I know."

Andrew was approaching, dressed quite unlike himself. Gone was his perfectly tailored suit, replaced with a kilt in the MacGregor tartan. His shirt—his tie was nowhere to be seen—was rolled up the elbows, showing up a perfectly matched set of well-muscled, lean arms. He looked a bit pink around the ears as he came to them, a hammer clutched in his own hands.

"Flora...might I have your favor?" he asked, holding out the handle to her.

Conner was leaning forward in his seat, watching them with interest.

Flora was so caught off guard by his response, she could hardly speak. She didn't think that he would be participating in any of the games, so she didn't bring anything to give as a favor. It wasn't as if she had planned on giving it to any of the Scottish men.

"Andrew," she began, feeling terrible that she would be sending him away empty handed. "I'm sorry, I didn't think to—"

Gwen reached up and plucked a decorative gray ribbon from Flora's bun and shoved it into her hand.

"Oh." Flora touched her hair, which now began to fall under its own weight. She had completely forgotten its presence there. "Thank you." Then she tied it around Andrew's hammer, her fingers trembling.

Andrew smiled down at her then turned to join

the other men, who didn't recognize him as an Englishman. With his dark red hair and plaid kilt, he looked the same as the rest—a true Scot. Flora wasn't sure why, but it made her rather uncomfortable to see him as...well, decidedly *not* him. She rather liked him as a gentle Englishman who favored books instead of a brutish Scot who lived by the blade.

"I say, what a turn of events." Charlie was almost shaking with excitement as he tugged on Flora's cloak. "Did you know he'd be going *full Drummond*, so to speak?"

"I had no idea."

"I suppose that's why he needed to talk to Drum," Gwen said, who began trying to salvage Flora's fallen hair.

Conner came up behind them, Ian perched on his shoulders like an excitable parrot. "What's the lad doin', then?"

"Isn't it obvious?" Flora shot back hotly. "He's throwing a hammer."

Her brother glared down at her. "This is no' a game, lass. He's wearin' tartan—"

"Supplied by Drum," Gwen cut in.

Conner ignored her. "And now he's out with the rest o' them, tryin' to look like one o' us?"

Flora would have punched Conner right in the sporran, if Ian wouldn't have fallen as well. "Honestly, Conner, you're being a terrible pest. Andrew has done nothing wrong and has been impeccably honest with everyone about his intentions toward me. He's getting into the spirit of the celebrations and is doing his best to befriend all of you. So you can take your negativity and shove it up your bloody arse!"

The area around them was quiet as Charlie, Gwen, Charlotte, Penelope, and a dozen other spectators turned to stare in her direction, agape in surprise. As Conner stalked back to his seat, Flora set her jaw and turned back to the event, where everyone was finally lined up, their hammers primed to throw. She found Andrew and focused on him, trying to quell the angry storm Conner had sparked within her.

She watched as the men raised their arms back. Andrew didn't seem out of step from the rest as he threw his hammer. It arched smoothly upward, made visible by her gray hair ribbon. Flora couldn't see where it fell, but waited with baited breath as a young boy ran out to see which hammer took first place.

The boy picked up a hammer with a red ribbon tied to the hilt and Big Angus called out, "It's mine!"

Flora felt an odd pang of disappointment that Andrew didn't win, although she knew he probably wouldn't. Big Angus was built like a beast of burden and he would probably continue to win at all manner of tossing games until he had his own giant son to take his place. But Andrew didn't seem to mind his loss either. He grinned as he approached her, his dimple on full display.

"I can't believe you did that!" she cried out as he stopped before her.

"I just went to the field. I was sixth out of twenty."

"That's wonderful." She reached out and squeezed his arm lightly, the way she often saw Penelope do to Drum. "I had no idea you would do the hammer toss. And that kilt! It's caught me completely by surprise."

"Yes, Andy," Charlie exclaimed, batting at Andrew's tartan hem. "Now tell us, what *do* you wear beneath your kilt? Flora is *dying* to know."

Flora couldn't speak; she merely closed her eyes and let out a deep breath of utter humiliation. Damn Charlie and his never-ending antics. But then a hand clutched her arm and began pulling her away from the events place and back toward the castle. It was Andrew. He stopped them just within the gate, only visible by the few maids and footmen who were preparing to set out a spread for supper.

"I'm terrible sorry for Charlie," Flora told him. "I keep telling him—"

She was suddenly silenced by his lips on hers. He pressed her against the cold wall of the keep, one hand beneath her fur cloak, wrapped tightly around her waist. She brought her hands up to his chest, feeling the muscles turn beneath her fingers. Flora could feel his heart beating wildly against her palms, echoing her own frantic one. She reveled in it before bringing both arms around his neck to pull him near. When Andrew coaxed her mouth open with his tongue, she complied.

Flora had been kissed before. She had kissed a stable boy as a child, then the son of a nobleman who once came to call on her eldest sister. And she had kissed Jasper, as loath as she was to admit it. But she had never been kissed in the intoxicating way Andrew was kissing her then.

His lips were soft and supple, but held a strong firmness that kneaded her own. She could taste the cider on his tongue and feel his hand drift up from her waist, skirting the line of buttons on the back of her gown, then moving toward her rib, stopping just below the curve of her breast. Flora knew what lust felt like. She relished the familiar feeling. But the sensation was made new by Andrew's constant adoration of not only her body, but her as person. It made their embrace the most intimate she had ever known.

When he drew back, his eyes dark with need and his lips parted, he gazed down at her with a look so full of longing, Flora felt her knees weaken. Her breasts rose and fell with each panting breath and she clutched his shoulders for support, grateful to feel them strong and firm enough to hold her.

"What…what was all that?" she panted, wishing she had the strength to ask for more.

Andrew's hands went down to her hips, then back up her waist, skimming the fabric of her dress with his long fingers. "I just…I needed to do that."

"And the hammer? The kilt?"

"I needed to do that, too." He leaned up against her, pressing his lips to her forehead. "I needed to show you that I am a man and not just a scholar."

Flora felt something press into her hip and thought he didn't need to show her anything to prove his manhood. She wanted to pull him close again and in the back of her mind she fought the primal urge to have him take her right there on the side of the keep. But she swallowed the feeling and covered it up with a small smile. "That's silly."

"It's not." He looked back into her eyes. "Among your people—your family—I'm just a learned man with soft hands. But I'm more than that and I'm capable of the things you're used to. I wanted to show you, and your family, that I respect your traditions and can live as you do."

"I don't want to live as the Scottish do, with my people. I want to live as the British do…with you." As soon as the words left her mouth, Flora wished she could call them back. Her presumptuous sentence hung in the air between them and she hardly knew where it had even come from.

Flora waited for Andrew to say something, but he stayed silent. Instead of answering her with words, he kissed her again. She could feel the outline of a smile on his lips as he did. This embrace was unlike the one before. It was softer, gentler, with the pangs of lust settling lower and the emotional need taking front and center between their breasts. But it made her heart race faster all the same. And when they parted, he still said nothing, but brushed his hand upon her cheek, wordlessly accepting her confession. Her confession of what, neither truly knew.

Then the caber toss was over and the revelers were approaching the keep again, Drum at the head, the obvious winner. Flora and Andrew broke apart, keeping a semi respectable distance. But as they sat with the rest of the clan at the long, wooden tables in the courtyard, Andrew's hand found hers beneath and they ate and drank and laughed with their fingers intertwined.

For the first night in a long time, Flora opened her window before she went to bed, letting the starlight and dreams stream inward.

Chapter Sixteen

When she awoke, a heavy shower of icy sleet was falling. Her bedroom window, which she had dreamily left open, had allowed a small, frigid puddle to collect on the stone floor. She guiltily shut the latch and threw a towel over the wetness, trying to sop up the water. Although her mother lived all the way down in the lowlands with her eldest sister, Flora could almost hear her chastising her for her negligence.

Then she donned a deep purple velvet gown and wrapped herself in a heavy wool shawl before brushing her hair and hastily pinning it up. The chill outside had seeped into the castle and she practically dashed down to the great hall, where the damp wooden tables and benches had been brought back in. The dozens of people and giant fireplace made for a toasty chamber, for which she was very grateful. Charlie, Gwen, and Andrew were nowhere to be seen. Charlotte and Penelope stood amongst a gaggle of women while Conner and Drum were at the head table, shoving their faces with fried eggs and slabs of meat.

"Good morning," Flora greeted politely as she sat.

"Mornin'," Drum replied, while Conner merely grunted. "Where's your man today, Flora?"

"He's not her man," Conner drawled, spearing a sausage with more force than necessary.

Drum shoved Conner roughly in the shoulder. "Do no' fash, Conner. We're only havin' a bit o' fun. Ye know, ye are no' much fun now that your wee sister has found a match. He's a nice lad, that Andrew."

"Ye do no' know that."

"But Flora does, and ye should trust her."

Conner looked from Drum to Flora with his lips tightly pressed. Then he heaved a sigh and left the table.

Flora felt the tension leave with him. "Thank you for intervening. It's much too early in the day for Conner's dramatics."

Drum shrugged and swallowed his bite of toast. "He'll come around. Ye understand why he is so vexed, aye?"

She did. She knew he feared another Jasper; another man who would use her for her station, her heart, her body, then leave her behind. But she knew that Andrew was different. Certainly many other young women said the same about their wayward paramours, but she could feel it in her bones that Andrew wouldn't cast her aside on a whim. No man would travel so far after being denied just to use and abuse her.

"And the plaid? What did ye think?" Drum asked

eagerly.

"I'm not sure I liked it."

Drum's green eyes widened. "Ye did no' like it? I dressed the lad in my own tartan."

"I know you did and I adored the sentiment behind it."

"But…?"

She looked down at her plate. "But I adore him as he is even more. If I wanted a Scottish man, I could have one…but Andrew doesn't need the brute force and clan backing to make him worth something to me."

Drum nodded, apparently pleased with her answer. He finished his food and left, leaving her alone. But not for long. A frazzled Gwen practically fell into his seat, the hem of her dress soaked and muddy.

"Everything is cancelled for the day." Gwen groaned as she was poured a cup of tea from the pewter pot beside her. "That spoils tomorrow's festivities and the bonfires planned for tonight. There were entire pigs that were meant to cook all day outdoors, and now the kitchens are positively overwhelmed.

Flora thought that Gwen needed a dash of something strong in her tea, and for the first time in days, she wished Charlie was there. Come to think of it, she hadn't seen him in some time, but him disappearing wasn't anything new. "It's all right, Gwen. Everyone's having such a good time indoors. Besides, there aren't many people staying overnight in the castle. Most are down in the village and won't need to be entertained by you today."

Gwen dropped her head to the table, which was how Charlie found her when he finally arrived. "Started on the drink early, have we?"

Flora shook her head. "No, but she should. She's rather stressed."

"We can't have that now, can we, my little golden child?" With a grand flourish, Charlie produced a flask from his jacket pocket and splashed something into Gwen's teacup.

"I can't," Gwen moaned, pushing it away.

"Well, I'm not having this go to waste." He pulled the cup toward him and swallowed it in one gulp. "Ah, yes. That should help my headache significantly."

"Should it?" Flora wasn't convinced.

"Honestly, you doubt my knowledge concerning the alcoholic arts?" He clasped his hands to his chest, his eyes raised to the heavens. "Dear Flora, you wound me!"

"Oh, stop it." She swatted his arm. "Have you seen Andrew?"

"No, I haven't." Charlie picked through the platters set before him, piling his plate with food. "I will say that there were two rather large men outside his door this morning when I came in to change."

"You didn't sleep in your own rooms last night?" Gwen asked, looking a bit scandalized, her eyes wide. "What of Penelope's cousin Matthew?"

Charlie sighed. "This story isn't about *me*, dear Gwendolyn, it's about Andrew. As I was saying, there was a pair of burly Scotsmen who appeared to have been there overnight. I invited both in for a nightcap, but they were somewhat uninterested in my offer."

"It was Conner," Flora mumbled.

"Oh no, darling, I would never invite Conner into my rooms." Charlie chuckled.

Flora rolled her eyes. "No, I was saying that Conner must have put them there. How positively ghastly. He doesn't trust either of us."

"Well, can you blame him?"

She narrowed her eyes. "I'm going to ignore that comment. Now, were they still there when you came down, just now?"

"No, they were gone."

Gwen nibbled the corner of a piece of toast and stood. "I suppose I should see how things are progressing in the kitchen. Come for me if anything happens."

Flora watched Gwen leave and disappear into the doorway that led into the kitchens below. Then she turned to Charlie, who was devouring his fourth egg. She was happy to finish her meal in their shared silence. It was very rare that she got a moment of peace, especially when Charlie was around, but she found his company comforting and sure. No matter his faults, he was always there when she needed him. But Andrew…

"I think I'll go for a walk," she announced suddenly, rising from her seat.

"I would offer to accompany you, but I know you're going off to find Andy." He dumped more sausage onto his plate. "I knocked on his door before I came down, so I don't think he's in his room."

Flora thanked Charlie then left the great hall, going to search for Andrew. On a hunch, she strolled through the corridors toward Conner's library. She pushed the door open and saw Andrew seated before the fire, a book in his hands. She stood there a moment, just watching him read. He was transfixed upon the volume, his brow slightly creased, and sometimes he mouthed the words, as if tasting them on his tongue. While not the shirt-ripping, sword-wielding, kilt-wearing men of her youth, his studious nature appealed to her greatly.

Flora let out a soft sigh and Andrew's eyes flickered to her. "Flora, I didn't see you there." She saw him slip her gray ribbon into the book to mark his place before closing it. She wasn't aware he had kept it.

"I wasn't here long. I just wanted to see if you were all right." Her eyes were still on the book. She thought it rather flattering he had kept something so small.

"Yes, why wouldn't I be?"

Flora sat down in the seat opposite him, her back straight, as Penelope's would have been, and her hands laid down gracefully in her lap. "Charlie told me there were men outside your room."

"Yes, but they didn't bother me. Your brother had told me he was having me watched and I really expected nothing less than an armed guard."

"That's so like him." She shook her head. "Reading anything good?"

He shrugged and placed it on the table beside him. "Nothing of great importance. Are you here for any book in particular?"

"No, I just came here…for you," she admitted. But realizing how odd that sounded, she said, "I mean, I just wanted to see how you were getting on in the castle."

"Quite well. Everyone has been exceedingly welcoming."

"I'm glad to hear it. And your rooms?"

Andrew smiled. "Is there something you'd like to speak to me about, Flora?"

"No, I'm actually just procrastinating to be perfectly honest," she admitted, thinking of Gwen down in the kitchens. "Gwen is probably wondering where I am, and the last thing I wish to be doing is cooking."

"Then I suppose this is as good a place as any to hide."

"She'll find me soon enough. Now that she cares for the accounts, she's in here a good amount."

"If she does spot you, I'll do my best to persuade her that your presence with me is necessary."

"On what grounds?"

"Cultural translation?"

"Since that will never work, at least tell me about the book you're reading. I need something fresh on my mind for when Gwen puts me to work."

"Certainly. Let's see…." He picked up the book and placed it thoughtfully in his lap. "This particular volume is on the Picts of ancient Scotland. Fascinating people, as you probably know. Well, this book only goes back…"

There was more, but Flora wasn't really listening. She was quite familiar with that specific book, as it was for her that it was originally bought.

What was really catching her attention was the way Andrew spoke with such confidence and warmth about such a bland topic. His voice was almost melodic and it comforted her to listen. She could easily imagine long nights by the fire in their own home, speaking of novels and him translating old texts and prose.

"You aren't paying any attention, are you?" Andrew asked, the corners of his lips rising.

"You've caught me." She giggled. "I was just listening to you talk...but not really, I suppose."

"How does one listen and *not* listen at the same time?"

Flora thought back to their initial meetings, when he stumbled over his words. "Might I ask you something that might be considered terribly rude?"

"Please do."

"When we first became acquainted at Penelope's...*event*, you spoke...well...you had a terrible stutter."

He groaned. "Oh, that."

"Yes, but it seems that it's gone. What happened?"

"I didn't ever have a stutter...not really, in any case." He looked down at the worn cover in his hands, his thumb brushing over the embossed gold of the title. "It's a terrible cliché, but I found myself utterly speechless in your presence. I thought of all sorts of interesting things I might say, but my mouth just couldn't keep up with my mind. You must have thought me a complete idiot."

"Oh, never."

Andrew raised a brow.

"Well, perhaps a little," she confessed, feeling rather guilty on judging him so.

"I'm glad to say that I've never been rendered completely incapable of forming a sentence before I met you."

"How flattering," Flora teased. Then she glanced at the clock on the mantle and sighed. "I really should go help Gwen. She didn't particularly order me to work, but I should be of more help to her as her sister." She stood and fluffed out her skirts.

He rose as well. "Shall I accompany you?"

"Heavens, no. I'm only going down as a show of good faith. If I'm lucky, she'll dismiss me on the grounds that my cooking is too terrible to be of any real help to her."

Andrew kissed her lightly on the cheek, sending Flora off with something pleasant to think of when she was elbow deep in pig meat and cow's blood. She strode back down the corridor feeling light. Everything was going well. Her family was healthy and happy, Charlie was visiting and actually helping things along for once, Gwen had found a purpose, and Flora was opening her heart to Andrew, allowing them to grow closer. She thought she might have actually found her happily ever after at last.

The feasting hall's closed doors were in sight when a hand shot out of an alcove and pulled her into the shaded corner. She opened her mouth to scream, but a palm roughly pressed against her lips, muffling the sounds. The man wore a dark woolen cloak, the soaked hem dripping onto the floor. His face was shadowed, but Flora knew at once who it was.

Jasper lifted his face into the dim light and smiled down at her. "If I lift my hand, do no' yell out."

Once his hand was removed, Flora tried to back away, but he still clutched her other arm tightly. "Jasper, what are you doing here?"

"I came back for ye."

"Conner said you would be killed if you returned to the Macleod lands."

"He won't—he *can't*. Everyone knows his wife would no' let him shed blood," he whispered eagerly. "We can be together."

"You're married," she spat, her heart racing with fear and anger.

"He released my wife from our vows. I am free to wed, Flora. We can marry and be happy!" He pulled her closer. "Ye get a bit o' land when ye marry, aye? We'll have a nice little farm, the two o' us."

Flora tried freeing herself, but the grip he had was too strong. She could feel his nails digging into her arm through the velvet fabric of her gown and knew there would be a bruise. "Please, let me go. You're hurting me."

Jasper frowned and loosened his hold a bit, but not enough for Flora to make an escape. She wished she had accepted Andrew's escort. None of this would have happened if he were with her.

"Can I go, please?" she begged, feeling tears well in her eyes. "Please, Jasper."

His eyes flashed. "Ach, lass…I love how ye say my name."

Jasper bent down and pressed his lips roughly to hers. His mouth was wet and harsh and smelled harshly of liquor. She tried to pull away, but her struggles seemed to excite him all the more and he deepened their kiss. Her sobs were choking her then and she beat her fists against his chest, but his time away from the castle hadn't ruined his muscular form and it was as if she punched stone.

When Jasper was finally ripped away from her, she fell to the floor, crying loudly with her eyes closed, clutching her shawl around her. It took her a moment to gain the courage to open her eyes, but when she did, she saw Jasper dazed on the floor and Andrew standing over him, a candlestick in his hand and his eyes wide.

Andrew dropped his impromptu weapon and dashed to Flora's side. "Are you hurt? Did he hurt you? Tell me!"

Flora couldn't speak. Only frightful blubbering came out when she opened her mouth.

"Come, let us find Conner." Andrew was about to help her up when Jasper regained his senses.

"Do no' touch my woman," Jasper croaked, rising unsteadily to his feet.

Andrew stood to face him, blocking Flora with her body. "How dare you mishandle this lady? She is the sister of the MacLeod."

Jasper laughed darkly. "Aye, I know who she is. I know much more than anyone else in this castle."

"I sincerely doubt that."

Flora tried to quell her tears and brought herself shakily up to stand.

"Flora, tell this man who I am," Jasper ordered,

pointing at Andrew.

"I don't care who you are. I am taking Flora to safety." Andrew grabbed Flora's hand firmly, but it didn't scare her, it gave her courage. "You assaulted her innocence, and that will not stand."

"Innocence?" Jasper mimicked with a smirk. "There is nothin' innocent about this lass. I had her already, so there's no innocence to ruin."

Flora fell back against the wall, dropping Andrew's hand. Her knees had given out and she resigned herself to sit on the floor and sob weakly into her shawl. Her greatest fears were coming true and she could do nothing to stop it. Her chance at love and happiness was being dashed before her very eyes.

"How dare you besmirch Flora's good name," Andrew growled in a tone Flora had never known him to have.

Jasper fingered the hilt of his dirk. "Like I said, I've already had the lass. I'm only tellin' what she already knows to be true. She came crawlin' to my bed like a common whore and—"

There was a sickening crunch as Andrew's fist made contact with Jasper's nose. Flora stifled a shriek as he dropped to his knees, clutching his face.

Then Andrew scooped Flora up like a bride and spirited her down the corridors until he came to the feasting hall. He kicked open the doors and his eyes darted around the room. "MacLeod!" he bellowed. "Where is the MacLeod!"

Conner appeared at their side almost instantly. "What the hell happened?!"

Andrew gently lowered her onto a bench before answering. "There was some man out in the corridor mishandling Flora. I think she's in shock."

"Was it one o' my men? Did ye recognize him?"

"I haven't seen him before, but she called him Jasper."

"That bloody...I'll have his head." Conner drew his sword. He was about to leave in search of his prey when the man entered, a grin on his face.

"Good day, MacLeod," Jasper crooned as he confidently strolled toward them, wiping the blood around his nose and mouth with a corner of his cloak.

"What are ye doin' here?" Conner roared. His sword hissed as he drew it from his sheath. "I spared your life and this is how ye repay me? Ye come back onto my lands and into my home and harm my sister?"

"I've only come to collect what I've already claimed."

"There is naught in my lands that belongs to ye," Conner told him sternly, brushing Charlotte's hand off his arm as she tried to latch on. "I did what I thought was fair, but now I know ye will only listen to blood."

Andrew leaned down beside Flora, his jaw tense and his fists clenched. "Are you all right?"

She nodded slightly and looked around at the silent feasting hall. Everyone was watching them, too interested—or frightened—to do anything else. She prayed Jasper wouldn't repeat what he had told Andrew in the corridor, but knew she could never be so lucky. If she had learned anything in the last hour, it was that nothing would ever stay a secret in her life.

"Ye've rid me o' my wife and I've already had the lass as a husband would, so why no' just make it official and bind us now?" Jasper crossed his arms over his chest, looking smug. "The only way to save her reputation is for me to marry her."

Flora thought she might be sick. Coercing Conner to agree to match by ways of copulation was originally her bright idea, but coming from Jasper's mouth, it seemed like a disgusting form of blackmail. And she didn't dare look at Andrew. Now he knew how used she was—tarnished and ruined. Flora knew he would be disgusted with her, but couldn't bear to see it in his usually kind eyes.

"How dare you," Andrew spat, drawing near to Conner and Jasper. "How *dare* you say those things about Flora? A lady of noble breeding and character!"

"Ach, ye know nothin' o' who she really is," Jasper said. "But I know her *inside* and *out*."

Conner lunged toward him, but Andrew beat him to it. The mild-mannered Englishman gripped Jasper's wet cloak with both hands. "I challenge you to a duel!"

"A duel?" Jasper repeated. "I'd spear ye in an instant, ye British fob."

"No!" Charlotte shrieked. "No killing."

Conner glanced at her out of the corner of his eye. The pair had a short, telepathic connection before Conner turned back to the crowd. "Aye, we can no' bring the stain o' death to Martinmas, as it would anger the old gods and the new. But I will no' wait to have ye fight, for I want Jasper gone at once. Ye may duel to first blood. And if ye lose, ye will be given to the ship captain that is currently docked at our port, guaranteein' ye will never return to Scotland. And as a final shame to ye, I'll have ye branded so all know ye can no' be trusted."

"And if he loses?" Jasper nodded toward Andrew. "I say *he* must leave Scotland and forfeit Flora's hand by official decree."

Conner looked between the two. "Done."

Jasper held up his hand. "*And* I want land. Good farming land with a big house to support my wee wife."

"No' my sister."

"Aye, your sister. She's the reason we're here. We fight for her."

Andrew shook his head roughly, fire in his eyes. "I will not stand for Flora being fought over like some manner of livestock. Wedding her in this manner for either of us would be cruel and ungentlemanly."

"Well, I am no gentleman," Jasper spat. "In a duel we can lay out our own terms and these are mine. She is the prize I want to claim."

"You speak of her with such distain and disrespe—"

"Ye know nothin' o' our ways, how we do things in the highlands. If ye no like it, then leave back to England."

Conner's knuckles were white as he clutched the hilt of his sword. "It is done. The terms are announced and the fight is set. No more will be said of the matter."

Flora gripped her seat. She saw spots before her eyes and fought the urge to pass out. She still couldn't speak. Her lips felt as if they were glued shut with terror and humiliation. Her old dream of forcing Conner's hand to allow her to marry Jasper was coming to pass. But now that dream had morphed into a sick nightmare and she could not awaken.

"Ye will fight at noon tomorrow," Conner announced before gesturing to Jasper. "Take him to the dungeons. Make sure he does no' leave."

Several men seized Jasper by the arm and began dragging him from the hall. Flora dared a glance in his direction, feeling sick as she saw that the smug smirk was still planted on his face. The rest of the gathering stared at her as if she were one of Conner's jarred specimens, pickled and set out for them to gawk at.

"Come," Charlotte whispered, holding out her hand.

Flora was still frozen in shock. She was aware of Conner's curses, Charlotte's concerned gaze, the crowd's low titters, Andrew's silent and blank observation. She wanted to run, run to the stables, ride to the train station, and leave Scotland behind for good. Yes, she wanted—*needed*—to flee, but couldn't will her fingers to loosen their grip on the bench or her legs to move.

Conner yelled something out to the gathering, but his words sounded muffled, far away. She couldn't guess what he said, but whatever it was sent the spectators back to their meals and hushed conversations. She could guess that conversations wouldn't be about the Martinmas events, but about her and the two men who would shed blood on the morrow.

A pair of strong, sturdy arms suddenly raised her up. They looped beneath her knees and behind her back. She looked up to see Andrew staring straight ahead, bearing her out of the hall. Flora waited for him to speak, but he said nothing, merely carrying her through the halls. His tarnished load to bear.

When they were almost at her room, and far away from any other person, she dared to open her mouth. "Andrew?"

He didn't respond. He opened her bedroom door and carried her over the threshold. Flora thought they made the saddest bridal-looking party in history. She thought it darkly amusing that she had hoped, in the deepest parts of her heart, that they would one day make that same journey as man and wife, but as ruined woman and hurt lover, it was far less romantic.

He gently set her down on her bed and pulled the folded quilt slowly over her legs. "Do you need anything?" he asked her in a tired voice. "I can have someone bring you tea or something to eat."

Flora was shocked anew. She had been revealed to be a harlot, yet he questioned if she required anything, as if she merely suffered from a common cold. His concern floored her. He had just been shamed before half the clan by association with her but her comfort and wellness was still his greatest concern. And he could die because of it.

She couldn't let him fight Jasper. Even in duels that claimed to end at the first drawing of blood, it was common for someone to be killed, no matter their opponent's intentions. And she wouldn't put it past Jasper to cheat, slicing an artery to bleed Andrew out, or spearing him clear though, claiming a slip of the wrist. What chance did a mild-mannered gentleman have against a seasoned warrior?

"Andrew...please...don't do it," she croaked, feeling hot tears begin their descent down her face.

"Do what?" He peered down at her, not in hatred or disgust, but something akin to sheer exhaustion.

"Fight Jasper."

"I must."

She shook her head. "No, you don't. Just call it off."

"I can't do that, Flora. I'm the one who called the duel."

"Please, just don't."

Andrew exhaled slowly then sat on the edge of her bed, taking her hand in his. "I must and I will. I need to defend your honor against such vile treatment."

Flora didn't know such a thing was possible, but she could feel her heart break at his confidence in her purity. It was like the slow, creaking lurch in her chest. She didn't deserve his pity. She only deserved his scorn and him leaving her for good, more for his own sake than hers.

"Andrew." Her voice cracked. "Andrew, Jasper didn't dishonor me."

"Of course he did. We all heard those awful things he said about you."

She drew her knees to her chest, hiding her face

in the blankets. The words she knew she should say were fighting to stay behind her teeth and she had to force them out. "He couldn't dishonor me because what he said was true."

Flora waited for Andrew to yell, to scream, to call her all those terrible things she called herself in her darkest moments. But he didn't do any of those things. He simply said two quiet words in the saddest voice she had ever heard.

"I see…"

Knowing whatever they had was over for good, she ripped her hand from his grasp and tore off the blankets. She thought she should tell Andrew goodbye, but couldn't bear the thought of saying those final words. In a terrible twist of fate, that was the moment her legs decided to cooperate. She leaped from the bed and scrambled from her bedchamber, letting her tears of sorrow and shame fall freely.

Flora didn't know where to go. Her family and the Martinmas guests milled through most of the castle…except Conner's library.

It was mercifully empty. Still, she couldn't risk the chance of begin found by a wandering guest or maid. If no one had been talking about her before, they certainly would have then. She climbed the stairs to the second floor of the library and sat down beside a case of ancient books, desperate to have a good, long, and interrupted cry into her skirts. But her moment of quiet was short lasting.

"Flora?" Andrew called out in the main library below. "Please, are you in here?"

She put her hands over mouth to stifle her tears,

but one small sniff escaped.

"Flora, is that you? Are you up on the second floor?"

There was no way she could sneak past him to the main castle. Luckily there was another way she could make her grand escape. She pushed open the door that led to a narrow corridor. Ahead was the exit to the balcony and to her right was a set of stairs. She turned for the stairs, but saw a coupled pair halfway down, their bodies unnaturally intertwined. She couldn't risk going by them either, as they were quite engaged and it was far too narrow to sneak past them. So Flora did the only thing she felt she could.

The veranda was three stories up, overlooking the keep's courtyard. The rain had lessened to a pitiful smattering of frigid drops, but the wind gusted, pressing her rapidly soaking gown to her body. Flora didn't feel the cold. She was already numb from the inside out.

She gripped the waist-high stone that kept her from falling to the courtyard below. Her tears blended in with the rain and the gale masked the sounds of her sorrowful crying. She was sorry she didn't think to immediately run outside. It was the perfect place to fall apart.

"Flora?"

She spun on her heel. Andrew stood on the balcony beside the door, his hair soaked and plastered to his face.

"Andrew." Flora wiped her face with her damp sleeve, not noticing how futile the motion was.

He stepped forward until he was right before her.

"Flora, come inside. You'll catch your death out here."

"I hope I do," she replied, half thinking of leaping from their perch. "Just leave, Andrew. Leave me and go live a good, clean life!"

"I can't live a good life without you in it," he shouted over the wind.

"All those things Jasper said about me are true," she admitted again, hoping to convince him to leave, for his own sake. "Every nasty thing!"

Andrew put one arm around her middle, his free hand cupping her cheek. "I don't give a bloody damn about that."

She was most startled to hear him curse than she was to feel his mercifully warm palm upon her face. "What did you say?"

"Flora, I don't care what you did before me. I don't care whom you were with or who you were. I don't care about Jasper. I don't care about scandal. I only care about who you are now and the life we can have together. I love you, Flora MacLeod. I love you more than some antiquated notion of purity, more than my studies, more than that bloody law practice with all those bloody boring men. You're the fire that keeps me sane and warm and I won't let you run from it, Flora. I won't let you stand here in the rain, extinguishing the flame that makes you *you*."

"Andrew—"

"Please, don't stop me now. I'm trying to make an impression on you and I can't have your dramatics spoiling it."

Flora went to speak, to tell him what she felt, but

he brushed his thumb over her lips, silencing her.

"If you want to live in Scotland and be a sheep farmer's wife, then get me a staff. If you desire a home in London in the fashionable side and a new hat every Sunday for church, you shall have it. I'll live where you want, how you want...I'll be who you want—"

"I want *you*!" Flora shouted at him. "I want you as you are, you stupid, stupid, *stupid* man." She laughed, the sound barely audible over the wind. "I want you today, tomorrow, *forever*."

Andrew drew his face close enough for Flora to see the beads of rainwater that collected on his long, dark lashes. Then he pressed his lips to hers and Flora poured all that she had into their kiss, running her hands over the soaked fabric of his shirt and holding onto their embrace as if she would fall to pieces without it.

Andrew's lips parted and he whispered, "Then I will give you forever."

Chapter Seventeen

Flora sat in bed with Gwen and Charlie both perched by her feet. Gwen looked positively shocked and Charlie kept murmuring about stabbing Jasper in his sleep. Flora and Andrew had gone to their respective rooms after their embrace in the rain and now she was bundled in several blankets, barely able to keep from sobbing.

"I can't believe Conner is allowing this," Gwen said quietly, toying with a loose string on the hem of her dress.

"He doesn't have a choice," Flora told her firmly. "Andrew called the duel and Conner can't stop it now, especially with so many witnesses."

"Bollocks," Charlie spat. "Isn't he some kind of king? Can't he just chop Jacob's head off or have him drawn and quartered?"

"Jasper," Gwen corrected.

"Yes, Conner should chop *Janice's* head off and be done with it," Charlie affirmed.

Flora pulled her furs up to her chin. "He can't do that either. Charlotte had him agree to stop executions in favor of humane punishment, especially as an execution has to be overseen by the courts of Great Britain. Then my follies would be fully public knowledge."

"We should poison him," Charlie suggested in a hushed voice. "Aren't there supposed to be all manners of witches in Scotland? Surely you have some sort of old crone you can call?"

Gwen shoved him lightly. "We can't kill people. Charlotte says it's not allowed."

"Which is why we poison him…no murder weapon. Honestly, Gwendolyn, what do they teach you in those fancy finishing schools for ladies?"

"Less about poison than you would think." Gwen turned back to the matter at hand. "But I do think we must do something. Jasper is very experienced with the blade and I wouldn't put it past him to fight dirty."

Flora felt her throat tighten. "That's exactly what I fear most. Should I, perhaps, talk to Jasper?"

"Conner has him under guard," Gwen told her, taking her hand. "The moment you go to the dungeon, Conner will hear about it in an instant."

"Surely Andy will listen to reason. He wouldn't wish to upset you." Charlie's voice was unnaturally soft, something that Flora found eerie.

"I think I'd like to rest now," she announced, turning on her side.

Gwen hopped off the bed. "Of course. Do you need anything?"

Flora shook her head.

Charlie was much slower to leave, but finally patted her on the leg and said, "I'll go see to

Andy…as long as you're positive that we cannot have Jasper poisoned?"

"I'm sure."

She waited until the bedroom door was firmly shut behind them before rising from bed. The floor was cold beneath her bare feet and she wrapped a robe around her as she paced before the fire. She usually found the sound of soft crackling comforting, but when the man she loved was less than twenty hours away from being slaughtered by the person she hated most, nothing on earth could ease her troubled mind.

Flora wasn't sure how to feel. She hadn't known Andrew that long, but she felt as if she was losing her life partner, making her a widow before she had a chance to be a bride. It wasn't fair. Andrew didn't deserve to die for her stupid misdeeds. And that thought made her furious. He was so determined, willing to die for her reputation instead of quietly slipping away to London, bringing her with him like she wished.

"Damn you, Andrew, you stubborn fool," she whispered, batting away the tears of frustration that dampened her already soaked cheeks.

She crossed to the foot of her bed, where her dowry trunk had sat since she was born. Every MacLeod girl had the same heavy, oak trunk and every year, their mother put something new inside for when they married. A set of silver baby spoons, ivory sewing needles, a book on maintaining a household…all lovingly selected for the future wives and mothers they'd been born and bred to be.

The lid was heavier than she remembered, and

she struggled to ease it open. The trunk was nearly full, packed tight with fine items. She sat on the floor and began pulling things out, inspecting each one and tossing it aside. It was therapeutic, in a way, to say goodbye to the gifts that were meant to be used in her marriage, for Flora knew once Andrew was gone, she would never love again. The finery was as good as trash.

One of the final things she pulled out was a series of packages wrapped in paper. Flora felt her cheeks heat. While most girls of her station would receive high-necked nightgowns for their wedding night, the grand Lady MacLeod held different standards and found the usual bridal garments to be bulky and unrefined. She prided in her collection of fine Irish lace from her homeland and she had ordered nightgowns and wrappers to be specially made for all her girls.

Flora carefully unwrapped both packets. The first held a fine silk robe in a luxurious cream. Delicate lace trimmed the edges and blue ribbon piped through the embroidery on the sleeves. The second package revealed a nightgown in the sheerest of chiffon with a daring lace neckline. As she fingered the two garments, she wryly thought it was a pity she would never wear them…that Andrew would never *see* her wear them.

"Wait a moment, Flora Fiona MacLeod," she muttered aloud, rising to her feet. "You are just as Charlie always says, *a delicate bloody flower*! If you want Andrew to see you in this sinful gown, then he will. And *then* he can try to tell you he'd give up being your husband to prove a bloody point!"

She began to laugh as she clutched the silks and lace to her chest. It was no secret to her that Andrew found her arousing. She had felt it herself as they kissed on the first day of the Martinmas celebrations. All she needed to do was seduce him into leaving Scotland for London and marry her at once. As soon as he beheld her form, he wouldn't dare dream of throwing her away in order to fight Jasper. She'd give him a reason to live, even if it was just her body. Then they would have a charming wedding in England and he'd be too busy with her in bed to think about ever drawing a sword again.

Smiling smugly, she dashed into her bathroom to begin her toilette. If she were to save Andrew's life, then she'd need to be perfectly irresistible.

***

The castle was silent when Flora stepped into the corridor, wrapped heavily in a cloak over her bridle negligee. A bag of coins was clutched tightly in her hands to use as a bribe for the guards outside his door. She had left her slippers behind, knowing she was quieter in her bare feet, and scurried through the halls. But she didn't meet anyone on her way and the men she thought she might meet outside his chambers where nowhere to be seen.

Once she was outside his door, Flora paused a moment to catch her breath and ensure her loose hair wasn't overly mussed by her cloak. It was strange that she should feel so nervous; it was not as if she was an untouched virgin and completely ignorant of the inner workings of the marital bed. But she thought that maybe her pounding heart had less to do with her purity—or lack thereof—and more to do with the fact that her actions might have the power to keep him from dueling. It was a lot of pressure.

She tapped lightly on the door, hoping that Charlie couldn't hear from his own chambers. This was one secret she didn't wish to share. After several louder knocks, she started to fear he wasn't in his rooms at all. That maybe, perhaps, he had taken her words to heart and fled for England. But that would mean he left her behind.

Feeling her heart begin to flutter painfully in her chest, Flora pounded on the door, mumbling, "That dratted man better not have gone and—"

The door swung open and there stood Andrew, a towel slung around his hips and his hair sopping wet. He initially looked rather vexed, but his expression softened when his eyes met Flora's in the dim light. Andrew looked down either end of the hall and then pulled her inside, locking the door behind her.

"Flora, what are you doing here?" he asked, brushing the wet locks from his eyes. "If your bother finds you here, then you needn't worry about my dueling, for he will spear me through."

She tried to find the words to answer him, but was left speechless by his naked torso. Of course she had been raised alongside bare-chested Scottish warriors, but seeing Andrew so exposed made her neck and cheeks hot. She couldn't look away. She had felt his form during their few, heated embraces, but now that every dip and curve of his muscular stomach and chest were so visible, she felt the urge to touch him. And as her eyes drifted downward, seeing the deep "v" that disappeared into his towel, she—

"Flora, can you at least pretend to be interested in what I'm saying?" Andrew was grinning rather broadly, obviously amused by her uncharacteristic speechlessness, but too polite to point it out.

She swallowed and averted her eyes. "I'm sorry, do continue."

He picked another towel off his bed and began drying his hair. "And I'm sorry for answering the door in such a state. With all that banging, I thought there was maybe a fire or some manner of emergency."

"No…just me…"

"Have you come to speak to me about tomorrow?" Andrew was at his wardrobe then, pulling out some clothes.

"Actually, I am." Her fingers worked away the clasp at her neck, dropping her cloak to the floor and baring her bridal robe.

He turned at the sound of fabric hitting the ground and nearly dropped his towel when he saw what she wore. "Flora…what are you doing?"

"Andrew, don't fight tomorrow," she said softly, taking several short steps toward him. "We can leave now and ride for the border. We'll be gone before the sun rises."

"I can't do that."

"You must." She took a deep breath, trying to

steady her voice. "Jasper is known to fight dirty. He isn't even allowed to spar and gamble in the surrounding villages anymore. Once, a few years ago, he *accidentally* stabbed a man in the heart during a blood duel. Do you know how difficult it is to slip your blade directly into someone's heart when you're trying? It's almost impossible to plunge through a set of ribs by accident. He won't fight fair."

"Well, *I* will. And I'll do what I can to honor you." He tucked a strand of hair behind her ear, his fingers lingering there. "Trust me, Flora."

"I came here to beg you, Andrew. Don't make me get down on my knees."

"You needed to come to me in your night things in order to tell me not to duel Jasper?"

"Did it work?" she asked in a voice she hoped sounded cheerful.

He shook his head. "Nothing you say or do will stop me from defending your honor."

"What good is my honor if you die?" Flora crossed her arms over her chest, feeling foolish and flushed at his serious manner and dismissal of her charms. "Jasper will fight dirty and I can't see you killed. I *won't*."

"And what good is *my* honor if I let some man speak of you in such a manner?" He bridged the gap between them, pulling her to his chest. "I know what I'm doing, Flora."

"No you don't," she spat, trying to stifle the sob that was threatening to come out. She had cried enough the past few weeks and couldn't stomach falling apart again. "Jasper's killed dozens of men and he'd kill you too."

"And I would die knowing that I did what I could for the woman I love."

"What good is your love if I have to bury you?" The drops of water from his dark red hair mixed with her tears upon his bare chest and she threw her arms around his middle. She had gone to him hoping she could seduce him out of Scotland, use her womanly allures to keep him alive. And there she was, crying into her chest in her useless French nightgown.

"You won't have to bury me," he murmured, stroking her hair.

She pushed away angrily, turning her back to him. "Of could I won't. I won't be *allowed* to, as we aren't wed. You'd be leaving me not a widow, but just some woman you died for."

"Which means more to me than a set of rings and a vow." Andrew came up behind her and pressed his lips to her shoulder. "Don't doubt me, Flora."

"I don't want to lose you." She softened under his touch and leaned back into him as he held her close.

Andrew nuzzled her neck and whispered, "You won't. Trust in me."

"I can't."

"Then lie and say you do."

She felt him smile against her skin. If that was his last wish, for her to act as if he could win, then she would do him that one favor. "Only if you promise to consider leaving tonight."

"I can't."

"Then lie and say you will."

He squeezed her tightly. "Look at us, lying to one another, just like an old married couple."

"You're not funny."

Andrew loosened his grip and spun her around. "But look, you're smiling."

She bit the inside of her cheek. "No, I'm not."

"I will say you look rather marvelous in this robe. Bridal white suits you."

Flora thought of her original intention and how it failed. But no matter what, she would leave his chamber as close to being his wife as she could manage. She reached down to the tie of her robe and let it fall open, exposing the sheer fabric and thin, lace straps.

"Flora," Andrew began, his gaze drifting downward. "What are you doing?"

She touched a finger to his lips to silence him and shrugged the robe off entirely, leaving her in the transparent gown. She knew she was being immodest, immoral, but she was already a ruined woman and at least she could say she bedded the man she loved. It was a small consolation for the realities of Andrew leaving his life. Before he did, he would leave his mark on her body forever.

"Flora, you don't have to do this." His hands were still at his side, one fist holding the towel, but she could see his fingers moving, as if he wished to put them to use.

"Andrew, I want to," she whispered, touching his chest, pressing her palm over his heart. "Don't you?"

His eyes raked her body and he took a deep breath. "More than anything…but we're not married."

"You said that didn't matter," she pointed out, looking up at him. "You said how you feel means more to you than rings and vows."

"Y-yes, but—"

She silenced him with a kiss, hoping he would abandon the fight and allow them to be joined. It worked. Andrew delved into the embrace hungrily, tangling his fingers in her hair and pulling her close. Flora let him ravage her lips, nip at her neck, and caress the bare skin of her back. It felt so different than the harsh fumbling of her one other sexual experience. Andrew was still gentle, touching each newly bared patch of flesh as if it were made of the finest china. She felt cherished and safe, firm that she was making the right decision.

When his fingers brushed against her breast, she moaned sharply into his mouth. Her own touched trails down the hard slope of his chest, over the ridges of his stomach, and further downward to his hips. The towel was tucked just tightly enough to keep it up, but she knew she could fell it with the flick of her thumb.

But before she could do so, Andrew scooped her up and carried her to his bed. "What kind of groom would I be if I didn't carry my bride?"

Flora smiled at being called his bride and ran her hand through his thick hair. She wished she had the beautiful declarations he deserved to hear, but every word she tried to speak died as it reached her lips. She was too overwhelmed to think of much more than the need to feel his body against hers and make their union as close to a marriage as she dared.

He hovered over her, kissing her forehand, her cheeks, the tip of her nose—every inch of bared skin, stopping short of the fabric of her nightgown. "You're so beautiful, Flora, but we don't need to do this to prove our love. I don't want you to feel pressured to do this tonight."

"Don't you want me, Andrew?"

"More than I've wanted anything in my entire life."

"Then help me get out of this." She began tugging her nightgown up, but Andrew averted his eyes when the hem hit her upper thigh. "What's wrong?" Flora felt a pang of self-conscious heat hit her in the chest and spread throughout her body. "Is-is it me?"

His gaze flew back to her. "No, Flora, not at all! It's just...I..." His ears reddened. "I've never seen...this is my first..."

A smile spread over Flora's lips. "So then help me out of it."

Andrew gulped and with shaking hands, slid the chiffon up her body, over her head, and tossed it to the floor beside his bed. He sat there for a moment, taking her in, his gaze brushing over her. Flora wished he would remove his towel, but didn't want to scare him. Instead, she pulled him down beside her.

"Touch me," she breathed, arching her back, offering him greater access to her form.

He ran his hand over her breast and along the smooth curve of her torso, coming to rest on her hip. Then his fingers repeated the movement back upward, circling her nipple. Flora let out a small squeal of delight as his mouth followed. For a man who had never seen a naked woman before, Andrew was setting her skin on fire with each slight movement and flick of his tongue.

When his lips finally traveled back to her mouth, Flora dared to tentatively grip the fabric slung about his hips. He didn't seem to notice, he was too busy lavishing her neck and breasts with attention. She slid her hand down and gripped his manhood, making him cry out in surprise. But as she moved her fingers up and down, his sounds of shock turned into ones of pleasure, and he held her tight against his chest, moaning into her mouth.

"I want you, Flora."

"You have me," she replied, releasing his member and wishing in the back of her mind that he would touch her in her most secret of places.

As if reading her thoughts, he slid his finger down to her delicate folds, exploring each inch. "God, Flora, you're so…so wet."

"More, Andrew, I need more!" She bucked her hips against his palm as he cautiously slipped a digit inside her.

He pulled away sharply. "Did I hurt you?"

"No!" Flora panted. "It felt good."

He moved to return his hand, but she moved it away, interlacing their fingers. "Now, Andrew. I need you in me."

"Are you certain?" He hovered above her, between her legs, rubbing his manhood against her slit.

"I love you, Andrew."

With that declaration he slid inside her, filling

her fully and sheathing himself to the hilt. They froze like that for a moment and Andrew pressed his lips to hers, smiling against her mouth. Flora ran her fingertips over the expanse of his back, craving his movement. She rose to meet him with each tender thrust, but it was still not enough. She craved more.

"Andrew, wait," Flora gasped.

He immediately stilled. "Are you all right?"

"Yes, get on your back," she ordered, feeling the need to take control.

Andrew complied, looking confused. But that look turned into one of delight when Flora straddled him, taking his member inside with one swift movement. One of Andrew's hands cupped her breast and the fingers of the other dug hard into her hip. Flora moved up and down with increasing speed, a delicious sensation building in her core. Andrew lay beneath her, watching her in rapture as she rode him.

But suddenly, he grabbed her by the waist and flipped her onto her back, still impaled on his length. Flora loved this change in demeanor; seeing a new, dominating side of him thrilled her. When he finally began thrusting, Flora bit his shoulder to quell the yell of pleasure that attempted to escape. Her teeth on his skin seemed to bolster his arousal and his movements quickened.

She clawed his back as he drove into her, moaning her name as he neared his own climax. The feelings of lustful desire began rising from the juncture of her thighs, spreading a carnal heat through her torso that shot through her limbs. Flora shouted, pleaded, screamed as Andrew entered her for the final times, before spilling into her all that he had and claiming her as his own.

They lay beside one another, the storms of passion ebbing into a gentle tide of completion that left Flora feeling warm and satisfied. She turned to her side, resting her head upon Andrew's chest. She listened to the slowing of his heartbeat, sighing as he wrapped his arms around her.

"Are you all right?" Andrew asked once he caught his breath. "I didn't hurt you, did I?"

"Of course not."

"Did…did you…enjoy yourself?" His voice was a timid whisper.

Flora kissed his chest. "Of course I did."

"Good." He sounded pleased. "I think I could do that every night for the rest of my life."

She was about to laugh, but stopped short. Flora had been so caught up in the moment that she forgot how they ended up in bed together in the first place. Her delirious happiness was replaced with the sickening stabs of fear that had pained her before.

Flora sat up. "Andrew—"

"I think I like you even better when your hair all mussed and your cheeks flushed." He grinned, running his hand down her arm. But his smile faded when he saw her welling eyes. "What's wrong?"

"Please, don't fight tomorrow," she begged. "Every night can be like this in *London*."

He took her hand and pressed his lips to her palm. "Flora, I asked you before to have faith in me that I wouldn't leave you an unwed widow. Trust me, please, and say no more."

"I can't, because I love you."

"Tomorrow is done and there's no running away. I'll ask you once more to believe me when I tell you that my love for you will see me through alive. Then I want to say no more of the matter and just look at you so I can remember you now, just as you are in this moment."

Andrew opened his arms and Flora meekly slid back down. If it was truly his last night on earth and all he asked was that she believe in him, she wouldn't spoil it with her tears.

"I have something for you," he told her after several moments of silence. "It's in my jacket pocket."

He made a move to rise, but Flora flattened her hand on his chest and pushed him back down. "Give it to me tomorrow," she whispered, holding tightly to him. "Give it to me tomorrow…after you win."

Chapter Eighteen

Flora stretched under the covers, smiling dreamily when her hand brushed up against something warm. She opened her eyes to see Andrew's sleeping face, lit by the early morning sunlight that streamed in through the gaps in the curtains. He looked to peaceful, lying there, his full lips parted, and his long lashes resting neatly on his cheeks. His auburn hair was gently tousled from sleep and hung over his smooth brow.

She pored over his features, taking in each line and angle. She didn't want to miss even the smallest freckle, in fear that it would later cause her to forget all that she had memorized. So Flora laid there, maybe an hour, maybe less, just watching the steady rise and fall of his chest.

"Good morning," Andrew whispered, making Flora jump.

"Goodness! You frightened me!"

He opened his eyes and pulled her close. "I'm sorry. I was letting you stare at me, but there's only so much a man can take."

Her cheeks burned. "I was just—"

"You needn't explain."

Flora threw her arm over his stomach, holding him tightly. "Andrew—"

"Please, Flora," he muttered, kissing the top of her head.

She bit her lip, trying to keep herself from more displays of displeasure. Instead, she focused on breathing him in, trying to learn each muscular curve that wrapped around her body. It felt perfect—it *was* perfect, the pair of them lying tangled in a warm bed, the bright sunlight illumining their intertwined limbs and a spiced fire filling the room with scents of nutmeg and cloves. Andrew brushed his fingers through her hair and she stroked the soft skin at the base of his neck, tracing his collarbone. She wished they could stay in that moment forever.

Andrew reached out a hand and picked up his pocket watch from the nightstand. "It's getting late."

"How long?"

"Less than two hours," he replied. "I need to prepare."

Flora didn't want to move, but knew she needed to give him time to dress, eat, pick his weapon, pray. "Yes, I should go dress as well."

She slid hesitantly from the bed and picked up up her sheer nightgown, tossing it on. Then donned her bridal robe, fastening it about the middle slowly, as to drag out their final moments. She slid her gaze toward Andrew. He was sitting up, watching her with a smile on his lips.

248

"You're beautiful," he told her.

Flora tried to smile in return, but it felt unnatural. "Thank you."

"You needn't come, if you can't bear it.

"I'll come. I must."

He nodded. "Then I'll see you in the parlor just before noon?"

"Yes."

"Wear something nice, for when I win."

Tears welled in her eyes and she stood there, clutching her cloak, wondering how on earth a man like Andrew could be in such a predicament. "I always do." She turned from him to hide her tears and scurried from the room, only letting the sobs overtake her when the door to her own chambers was sealed shut.

***

Flora stared at her reflection in her dressing table mirror and patted more powder on her flushed cheeks and on her puffed under-eyes. She didn't want Andrew to see that she had been crying, for she promised him she would not.

Her midnight blue gown felt like a burial shroud and her addition of a black lace choker and dark fur cloak did little to help the matter. But she felt like the walking dead, although Andrew's blood would not be the only spilled that day. A *sgian dubh*, a small dagger, was strapped high to her thigh. A hidden slit in the skirt of her dress would make for easy access to the perfectly sharpened blade when Jasper came for her.

249

"Flora, are you ready?" Gwen asked from the doorway, already clad in her own cloak.

She nodded and stood, leading the way down to the main floor of the castle. Gwen followed mutely, and Charlie joined shortly after, with Drum and a pale Penelope leading up the rear. She felt rather like some manner of warlord, leading her ragtag army to battle. She hid the shaking of her hands in her cloak.

Andrew stood by the main doors, heavy in conversation with Conner. She saw that Andrew held her brother's personal sword in his grasp and couldn't decide if that was good sign or not. But after a moment's deliberation, thought there wouldn't be a finer sword in Scotland, for Conner took immaculate care of his weapons.

"Flora," Andrew said as she approached.

She paused a moment, taking in his sober face and pursed lips. "Are you ready?" she asked in a hoarse whisper.

He nodded. "Are you?"

"No. But I'll have to be, because I love you."

Andrew's jaw tightened and he pulled her to his chest, crushing her in his embrace. He didn't say the words back, but Flora knew his actions said far more than a single phrase could portray.

When he released her, he gave her one last, longing look, then strode up to Conner, who clapped him on the back before leading the procession from the castle. Flora glanced around at the silent party. Charlotte was beside Conner, wrapped in her tartan, but lacking baby Alec, for which Flora was glad. Charlie was grim faced and green about the gills and Gwen's blue eyes flashed as she reached out and grabbed Flora's hand. Flora was glad for her fierce little sister's support, although the fingers of her free hand ran over the series of small sapphires on her dagger's hilt.

When they reached the cliffs overlooking the ocean, the theater for the duel, Jasper was already there, Big Angus standing sternly at his side, obviously displeased at being made his guard. There was a small congregation of men and women who had been at the keep for the celebrations there as well, their earthy hunting plaids blending into the rocks and hills around them. Their faces were grave and many sets of eyes dashed in Flora's direction. Their attentions made her blush, but she stood stalwart, the picture of a strong Scottish woman.

Jasper tried to grin at her, but Flora turned toward the ocean. There she saw a large ship anchored in the dark water, in line with the short strip of beach that sat two miles away at the foot of the cliff. It bounded with each crashing wave and its half drawn sails billowed lightly with the wind. She knew it to be the Portuguese trading vessel that she prayed would take Jasper far away from Scotland.

"Ye come here to fight this day to the first blood. No one shall die, but as soon as one o' ye is cut, the duel will be over and the punishments and rewards, dealt," Conner announced, his voice booming over the crashing waves below. "Andrew Philips, ye fight for Flora MacLeod's honor and for the right to make her your bride."

Flora jumped a bit. Marriage wasn't mentioned in the original announcement. She assumed that was what the men were whispering about in the entryway, but focused more on the task at hand. She couldn't waste any precious energy thinking of what could have been. If Jasper killed Andrew...she couldn't think of it. Instead, Flora kept her eyes trained on Andrew and counted the jewels on her dagger.

Big Angus passed Jasper a plain, but well-kept sword that she knew was from the armory. It seemed no one wished him well in his venture, because none of them offered him use of their own weapon. In a petty way, Flora was glad that the clan had turned their back on Jasper and hoped his blade was cursed.

"Are ye both ready?" Conner asked, backing into the crowd to give them ample space to spar.

"Aye, let us be done with it," Jasper snapped, a sly grin spreading over his face as he threw off his shirt. He then unsheathed his sword, tossing the scabbard to the ground and crouching low, recoiling on the balls of his feet, his eyes sharp. "I'll have this lad bled in a moment."

Andrew said nothing at first, just unbuttoned his fine English shirt and passed it to Charlie, then drew his borrowed blade, the sheath also being set aside, albeit carefully. He tested the weight of the blade for a moment, his face unreadable. Then he stepped back, his left leg slightly behind and the sword held firmly within his grasp. The weapon barely shook as he stood there and is seemed almost like an extension of his outstretched arm.

"Ready," Andrew stated clearly, his eyes trained on Jasper.

Conner paused for only a moment before calling out, "Begin!"

The swordsmen clashed in an instant, the sound of steel on steel reverberating in Flora's chest and the surrounding hillside. The spectators stayed frozen as the men fought, Jasper stabbing and slicing in the air as Andrew deftly slapped away each of his blows, his feet dancing from side to side as he nimbly weaved and bobbed.

"I had no idea…" Flora was flabbergasted. Andrew had never told her he was a skilled swordsman, but he seemed perfectly matched with Jasper as his partner, although they could not be more different. Where Jasper was rough and thick with jabbing blows, Andrew was lithe and lean, skirting the assaults almost gracefully. For the briefest of moments, Flora wondered if Andrew could really win.

Flora clutched Gwen's hand tighter as Jasper nearly stabbed Andrew with a sharp swing. But he dodged it neatly, slapping away the blade with a scooping motion that left both of Jasper's hands empty. The sword fell, arching through the air and falling to the ground several feet away. Andrew then reached forward and cut Jasper's upper arm with the tip of his weapon, causing a small ribbon of blood to paint his skin.

"It is done," Conner bellowed at once. "Andrew Philips has drawn first blood, leaving him the winner. Jasper MacNee, ye are—"

"No!" Flora shrieked as Jasper fell upon Andrew, who had been looking in her direction. "Andrew!"

The pair tumbled to the ground where, after a short scuffle of fists and feet, Jasper sat atop Andrew, who grappled to steal his sword. Jasper had the weight advantage then. While Andrew was lighter and faster upon his feet, Flora could see him struggle to breathe as Jasper held his throat with one hand and grabbed for the blade with the other.

"Conner, do something!" Flora begged. She made a move to run to Andrew, but Drum's large arms grabbed her around the middle and held her tightly to his chest.

"Do no' go, lass," Drum murmured as Flora fought to free herself. "The lad must do this himself and no good will come o' ye gettin' in the thick o' it."

She allowed him to hold her, but still felt her heart lurch with each terse moment. Flora watched as Jasper grabbed the sword's blade, now with both hands, pushing it downward towards Andrew. Drops of blood from his palms splattered upon Andrew's bare chest and she could see him struggle to keep the sword's edge from slicing into his flesh.

The men were both pink cheeked with effort as they struggled over who would gain total control of the single weapon. Flora was glad for Drum's support as they watched the final moments of the fight. She felt her knees weaken as Jasper pushed harder, now balanced on his knees. But in one smooth arch, Andrew thrust the blade upward, slicing through the skin at Jasper's neck, bearing his throat open.

Flora screamed in both release and alarm when Jasper's blood sprayed over Andrew, coating him in a wash of red. Jasper's body then heavily fell atop Andrew, who was just as immobile as his dead counterpart. She wondered where the sword had landed once it drew Jasper's life from him, but she was still encased in Drum's firm embrace.

The crowd stood stiller than a circle of standing stones as they waited for either Jasper or Andrew to move. But neither did. Both laid there motionless and the only sound Flora could hear was the rough waves hitting the rocks below and her own heartbeat in her ears like a funeral march.

Conner was the first to step forward. His mouth a hard line, he lifted Jasper's body by the hair and tossed him to the side, causing a fresh wash of blood to seep from the open gash. Then he crouched beside Andrew's form and leaned down. From a distance, it looked as if Andrew's lips were moving and Conner was listening intently, but Flora couldn't be sure.

"What is it? Is he all right?" Flora called out, fighting once again for Drum to release her. "What did he say?"

Conner looked up and his mouth split into a grin. "He said the bastard was so heavy, he knocked the wind right out o' him!"

Flora let out a cry of relief as Conner gripped Andrew by the blood-covered arm and lifted him up, clapping him in the back. Andrew took a deep breath and scanned the crowd until his gaze found Flora's. Drum released her then, and she bounded toward Andrew, tears falling freely down her face in sheer relief.

She flew into his arms, crashing hard against his

255

chest. But after a moment, Andrew held her at length. "Flora, as much as I'd love to hold you, I'm…covered in…" He motioned to his red torso.

"I don't mind," she said in earnest. Flora would never take an embrace for granted again.

"I-I'd like to go…" He cleared his throat, peering around at the spectators, who were still watching in interest. "I'd like to go clean up…"

"Oh, goodness, I don't want to keep you here like this. You're so right." She worried over him, holding tightly to his arm, staining her dress with the rapidly drying blood. His concern over his own cleanliness gave her something else to worry about, other than her own mixed emotions. "Hurry, come into the castle and we'll clean you up. Are you hurt? None of that if yours, right?"

"No, Flora, none of it is mine." His gaze slid over to where Jasper lay, but Flora pressed her hand to his cheek, forcing him to look her in the eye.

"I'm glad of it, Andrew," she told him fiercely. "You're a brave man."

Conner came beside them, but Flora shook her head, motioning for him to retrieve his sword. Then she continued on her task of taking Andrew to the keep. She saw his hands were shaking, so she grasped one in her own and held it tightly, ignoring the sticky blood now coating her palm. Charlie followed, still quiet. His silence still unnerved her, but she had little to fear, since Andrew was alive and well.

When they passed through the gates and into the courtyard, anyone who didn't go to the duel stopped and stared. The party of three—now four, as Gwen had hurried after them—quickened their pace, speeding though the hallways and stairs until they came to Andrew's door.

"Go get cleaned up," Andrew told her quietly, pressing the back of her clean hand to his lips.

"Do you need my help?" she asked. His fingers still shook and there was a darkness to his gaze that worried her. She didn't want to leave him alone.

He glanced at Charlie. "No, it's all right. Charlie promised me a drink, didn't you, Charlie?"

Charlie's red brows disappeared into his hair. "Oh...oh, yes!" he exclaimed with forced glee. "I told Andy I would liquor the old chap up. Drink, drink, drink! Ha-ha!"

A choked sort of chuckle shot from Gwen's pursed lips as Charlie broke into hysterical laughter that was both ridiculous and terribly forced. Flora took it as her cue to leave and squeezed Andrew's arm one final time. He brushed his hand over his bloody face.

"You'll be all right?" she asked in a whisper.

The corners of Andrew's mouth lifted. "Yes, will you?"

"Now that I know you're alive and well, nothing can spoil anything anymore."

He kissed her knuckles again. "I'll see you soon."

Once Charlie and Andrew had disappeared into the room, Gwen and Flora made the short journey to her chambers. When the door was safely latched, Flora allowed herself to fall to the stone floor. She had pretended to be brave for Andrew's sake, but seeing his body that just hours before had held her so tenderly, covered in blood, chilled her. It was confusing to feel so frightened and relieved at the same time. She took big gasping breaths as Gwen nimbly undid her gown and scurried into the bathroom to fill the porcelain tub.

Left only in her shift, Flora shambled to her dressing table and sat down before the mirror. She went to take off her choker when she caught sight of herself in the mirror. There was a smear of red down her cheek and her arms were covered in Jasper's blood. She felt the urge to be sick, but closed her eyes, trying to focus on her breathing.

"Shall I help you?" Gwen's voice was quiet, but even-keeled.

Flora couldn't open her mouth, so she merely nodded, allowing Gwen to remove her necklace then half carry her to the washroom, where Flora disrobed. The bath was hot and smelled of her favorite eucalyptus scent. Gwen pinned up her hair and she sank deeper into the fragrant water until her shoulders were submerged.

Gwen picked up a washcloth and began wiping her face. "Would you like to talk about it?"

"I-I don't know if I can," she rasped. Flora didn't know how to feel and didn't want to dump her mixed emotions on her little sister's lap.

"You should try."

"Well…well, I feel relieved that Andrew wasn't injured," she began, staring at her knees through the water. "I feel…proud in a way that he fought so valiantly for my honor. But I also feel ashamed that he had to in the first place. If I hadn't…done what I did with Jasper, Andrew would have never been put in this position."

"Anything else?" Gwen asked as she turned to get a fresh towel from the linen closet.

Flora bit her lip, her mind flashing to Jasper's dead body, lying near the cliffs. "I feel guilty…guilty that those two men fought over me. And guiltier still that Jasper, a man I thought I loved, is dead and I can only feel relief." Her voice cracked. "And now I don't even know why I'm crying!"

"You've been through a terrible shock. You're allowed to cry."

"I don't want to cry," she sobbed. "I just feel so terrible and I wish none of this had ever happened."

"But it did and now it's over. Jasper is gone and Andrew killed him for your honor. He was so brave today, and now you must be for him."

"You're right. I need to pull myself together. I can't be a blubbering mess! Andrew did something amazing today and here I am, making it about myself." She splashed some water on her face, washing away the tears. "I need to wear something brilliant and go to Andrew and be the woman he deserves."

"That's the Flora I know." Gwen smiled. "Now, let's get you ready. I'm sure the cook will prepare something marvelous for dinner."

***

When Flora was dressed in a pale blue gown, pearls at her ears and throat, Gwen pronounced her fit to see Andrew. So she donned her white slippers and hurried to his chambers, ready to show him how much she appreciated all he had done. But when she rounded a corner, she slapped hard into Charlie's chest.

"Oh, I'm sorry," she said, fluffing out her skirts. "I was just going—"

"To see Andrew, obviously." Charlie took a long swallow from his flask. "But he isn't in his room. And I must say, you Scots truly know how to have a wild party."

"Not funny."

"I'm being honest. No one ever gets killed at a London bash."

Flora rolled her eyes. "You're so dramatic. This isn't something to make light of."

Charlie's mouth flattened. "Trust me, I know. Andrew's taking it rather hard at present."

"What's happened?"

"He just feels...well, I'll let him explain it to you."

"Really, Charles?" She balled her hands on her hips. "You're always the first to announce the slightest bit of gossip and now you've nothing to say?"

He shrugged. "For once, I wish I didn't."

"I'm sorry." Flora sighed. "You're right. I'm just worried about Andrew. Do you know where he is?"

"No, he just said he was out for air. But I hope he didn't go far. It's snowing now," Charlie told her as he continued on his path.

Flora stepped over to the hall window overlooking the courtyard. A light dusting of white covered the walls and ground outside and more snow was lightly falling, adding to the frost that edged the glass. She couldn't see into the hills, but thought Andrew wouldn't go out into unfamiliar territory, particularly when he would have to pass the place where he felled Jasper.

She had a sudden thought, remembering how she had hid from him on the balcony above the library. She hoped she was right, as she walked through the halls, garnering her strength. Andrew deserved to hear something from her—an apology, a declaration of love, something to make his life a bit brighter, and something to help him forgive her for everything she had done that had led them there.

"Andrew?" she called out quietly when she stepped into the study.

When no one answered, she stepped though the carpeted room, her slippers silent. Then she climbed the stairs to the second floor, peeking into where she had first hidden from him days before. She took a deep breath before going into the narrow hallway and opening the heavy oak door to the balcony.

Andrew stood facing the sunset, his back to her. His hands were deep in the pockets of his jacket and the shoulders were covered in a light dusting of snow. Flora stepped out onto the stone, the frost below her feet crunching lightly with each step. He didn't turn as she approached him, but when she gently laid a hand on his arm, he looked down at her. She was pleased to see that he was bathed and freshly shaved, dressed in clean clothes.

"Flora, what are you doing out here?"

"I could ask you the same question."

He shrugged off his coat and draped it hurriedly

over her shoulders. "You're going to catch your death."

"I had to come find you." She wrapped her arms around his waist, pressing her cheek to his chest, relishing the steady beat of his heart.

He gently stroked her back, resting his chin on the top of her head. "Are you...are you afraid of me now, Flora?"

She pulled back, almost alarmed at his question. "What?"

"Well...I...I killed a man, a man you once cared for." Andrew looked away. "I slaughtered him before your eyes."

"And I'm bloody glad you did!" she told him sternly. "I'm glad he's dead and you're not. I'm glad you're standing here safe in the freezing cold instead of him."

"I've just never killed anyone..." His voice was softer, almost unsure of his own words.

Flora's heart broke for him. She remembered when Conner was young, twelve years old, and he'd gone riding with their father. He had stabbed a man who attacked them, killing him before he hit the ground. Her brother spent the evening crying into their mother's skirts. Flora never told anyone she'd seen him in such a vulnerable position, but she remembered it all the same.

She reached up and placed her hands on either side of his smooth face, his coat slipping from her shoulders. "Andrew, he would have killed you, had you not defended yourself. You did the only true and right think you could have done and he deserved to die. I know you didn't want to be the one who dealt that kind of punishment, but you did it for me and I love you for it."

He drew his head down, touching his forehead to hers. "I'd do anything for you, Flora."

"I know that." She gripped the collar of his shirt and pulled him into a deep kiss, one they had been waiting for since the duel.

They clung to each other, drinking each other in. Andrew's teeth nipped Flora's lips and she tangled her hand in his dark auburn hair. His jacket fell to the ground and the snow swirled around them like an icy tornado, but neither felt the flurry, only the warmth emanating from their intertwined bodies.

"God, Andrew, I'd have you take me right here if it wasn't so cold." She giggled into his lips as they parted. "Let's go inside. We'll warm up in your chambers." Flora wanted nothing more than to feel his hands upon her skin.

He looked as if he might have wanted to move, but he didn't. "Flora…"

She cursed herself. She had been too forward. "I'm sorry, that was inappropriate of me."

"No…it's not that…*never* that." His gaze fell to his jacket, which was still lying on the floor.

"Oh, goodness, how careless of me!" Flora belt down to retrieve his coat and brushed the snow off, vaguely wishing that it had never fallen to begin with. Her teeth were beginning to chatter. She passed the jacket back to him and he immediately dug through one of the pockets. "Is something amiss?"

"Yes. I mean…no," he muttered, until his fist closed over something small. He draped the coat over the short wall and turned to her. "You love me, Flora, yes?"

"You know that I do."

Andrew dropped to his knee in the snow and lifted up a small, black, leather box. "Flora, I've loved you from afar as a beautiful lady I could never dream of obtaining. Then I loved you as a funny, Scottish lass who always kept me guessing. And I love you more now as we stand in the snow that will always remind you of your home as I take you back to mine."

"Andrew…"

He flipped open the box's lid to show her a stunning ruby, held by a pair of delicate golf thistles. "Flora, I love you most ardently, most purely, and will continue to do so for the rest of my life if you agree to marry me."

Flora felt tears prick her eyes for the hundredth time that week, but for the first time, it wasn't out of fear, humiliation, or grief. But joy.

***

As they lay together, twisted atop her bed covers, Flora stared at the stunning gem upon her ring finger. She pressed her lips to his neck and whispered, "You did a marvelous job selecting this."

"I'm so glad you like it," he told her, brushing her tangled hair away from her face. "But now you must give it back."

Flora balked. "What?"

He nodded grimly. "Yes, this ring is only for my

bride, which you never agreed to be."

"What do you mean?" She motioned down to their nude bodies. "We're in bed together."

"Yes, I showed you this little bauble and you practically dragged me down the stairs into your chambers and ravished me," he declared with a sigh. "I'm quite scandalized."

Flora giggled, giving him a small shove. "I assumed that my actions meant that I accepted your proposal."

"Without a definite acceptance, how am I to know your true thoughts?" He skimmed his fingers over the curve of her shoulder and around the modest swell of her breast. "Without a resounding yes, we're merely lovers."

"You say that like it's a bad thing."

He kissed her lightly. "Nothing with you can ever be bad."

"Now, tell me about this wonderful ring. It looks as if it has a marvelous story to tell." She held it up, the lamplight casting a pleasant glow. It felt as if she was holding a flame in her grasp.

"Well," he began, taking her hand and lacing his fingers with hers. "I purchased this ruby from a lovely little jeweler. Cost an arm and a leg, but I told him that I could only have the best for my fiery Scottish lady."

"Is that what you called me?" she asked with a wry smile.

"Isn't that what you are?" When Flora didn't answer, he continued, "That jeweler didn't do the kind of work I wanted for the band, so I brought the stone with me to Scotland."

"You did?"

"I did. When we reached Edinburgh, I took it to a master of fine jewelry one of my uncle's clients knows. He was able to help me select this band for you. I wanted you to have a piece of Scotland wherever you went. So now you have an English ruby and a band of Scottish gold."

"A blending of two worlds," she noted, looking at their interlocked hands.

"A blending of our worlds," he replied, pressing his lips to the stone before moving on to the delicate skin of her neck. "Now, Flora, about that *yes…*"

Epilogue

Flora watched Gwen pace with interest. Her little sister looked oddly vexed in a way she hadn't seen for quite some time. Her blonde curls bounced around her flushed cheeks as she turned back to Flora and finished sticking sprigs of orange blossoms into her braids.

"You're looking awfully irritated," Flora said as Gwen muttered something under her breath in Gaelic. "You never speak *Gàidhlig* unless you're particularly upset or scared."

Gwen frowned and adjusted Flora's veil before pinning it onto her looped hair. "I'm sorry. You're the one getting married. If anyone should be acting like a brat, it's you. So, tell me, are you frightened that you'll be walking down the aisle in less than an hour?"

"No, no, I want to hear why you're stomping about like a child. It's rare you throw such a fit." Flora welcomed the respite of all attentions being on her. Normally, she would relish the constant petting, but it was beginning to overwhelm her.

"Well, the Portuguese trader tried to short me," Gwen explained, leaning over the dressing table to dab a bit of rouge on her cheeks and lips. "He came late last night to deliver cases of Italian wine for your wedding, among some other frivolities, and tried to short me."

"How so?"

"Well, each lot was to be bought for seventy-two pounds each, as each bottle was twelve pounds and sent as cases of six. As our men were loading them into the carts this morning, one remarked that Italian wine was much lighter than the French. Well, I marched right up—"

"You were there?" Flora couldn't imagine her tiny sister bossing about a bunch of men, but then again, she had seen stranger things.

"Of course I was! I needed to ensure everything would be perfect. And so I ordered one be opened. The Portuguese weren't too thrilled, but one of our men did and I saw a bottle was missing! They had repacked the cases in sets of five, while still charging the seventy-two pounds." Gwen's eyes flashed. "The gall of those Portuguese. Well, I told their captain—"

"Their captain? Is he wildly fierce with a big beard?" Flora asked, wondering if he was anything like the pirates she had read about in novels with a peg leg and pet monkey.

She shook her head and her cheeks pinked again, noticeable even through the rouge. "No, his name is Gaspar Florencio and he's terribly young. Perhaps Conner's age."

"And tell me, what did you tell Captain Gaspar

Florencio?"

"I told him that he had best right the wrong done to our house or I'd have his hand cut off for stealing and his ship burned."

Flora gasped, stunned at her sister's harsh sentence. "Dear Lord, that's rather extreme."

"No one spoils your wedding day, Flora."

"I believe you." Flora giggled, still slightly shocked at her sister's demands. "So, did he right his wrong, or is there a burning boat in the sea?"

"We now have eighty bottles of wine, several rolls of silk, and he even sent some select pieces of jewelry as a wedding gift for you," she announced proudly. "Now, we must get ready to have you wed. You've made Andrew wait nearly four months."

"I needed to have orange blossoms and it was the fastest I could have them readied in London for Charlie to fetch."

"You delayed your wedding for a flower?" Gwen laughed.

Flora stood and began to shake out her skirts, feeling a bit embarrassed. "It's considered good luck in England to have orange blossoms. We're already being wed in the highlands in our family's chapel, but I wanted to be a British bride for Andrew."

"He makes you happy, doesn't he?"

"Of course he does, you little nitwit," Flora shot back with a grin.

"There are my two favorite wee lasses!" Conner bellowed as he opened the door to the small room attached to the chapel.

Gwen glowered up at him. "Conner, Flora could

have been getting dressed!"

"Do no' fash, she's already in her gown! There's naught to fuss over. Besides, shouldn't ye go find a husband in the crowd? Lord knows one o' my lasses, or my men if ye count Drum, gets married off at each weddin'." Conner leaned over and kissed Flora on the cheek. "Ye look lovely, Flora."

"Thank you, Conner." Flora took one last look in the dressing mirror, adjusting the sheer sleeves that covered her arms.

"Stop fussin', lass. Ye look like a right English rose in that dress," Conner said, holding out his arm for her to take.

Flora looked up, seeing that Gwen was already gone, away to take her seat at the front of the church. She took a deep breath and scooped up her bouquet of orange blossoms and white winter roses. Conner led her from the room and into the small alcove before the double doors to the chapel. It was strange to think that just a year ago, she had helped Penelope ready herself in that same church, and there she was, preparing to become Mrs. Philips.

As soon as a set of page bows opened the heavy doors, the organist struck up a wedding tune and Conner and Flora began their walk down the aisle. The pews has been strung with ivy and white flowers, and she could see the faces of those she loved as they passed—Andrew's parents, Charlie, Penelope and Drum, Charlotte with baby Alec, her two elder sisters with their husbands and children, her mother weeping into a white handkerchief, and Gwen, beaming at her from the front of the church.

Then her gaze fell upon Andrew. He stood

before the altar, the stained-glass windows enveloping him in an otherworldly glow. His dark red hair was brushed off his forehead and he smiled fondly down at her as she approached, his dimple on display. She could almost see him bouncing as she took the final steps to his side alone.

The priest cleared his throat as Flora passed her flowers off to Gwen and Andrew took both her hands in his and gave them a gentle squeeze. Once the guests had stopped all whispers of good wishes and compliments, the ceremony began.

"Ladies and gentlemen," the priest began in heavily accented English. "We come here this day to join together Andrew Thomas Philips and Flora Fiona MacLeod in the bonds of holy matrimony. At the bequest of the couple, I have been asked to make the vows as short as their courtship, but as meaningful as their love."

The crowd tittered in interested approval.

The priest turned to Andrew. "Andrew, do you take this woman, Flora, to be your lawful wedded wife in sickness and in health, for richer and for poorer? Do you swear to be true to her every day of her life, to pray for her, to worship your marriage, and to hold true these vows which you take today?"

"Always," replied Andrew, his gaze fixed upon her.

"It's *I do*, lad," the priest informed him in a loud whisper.

Andrew grinned. "I do."

"Better." The priest nodded and turned his attention to Flora. "Flora, do you take this man, Andrew, to be your lawful wedded husband in

271

sickness and in health, for richer and for poorer? Do you swear to be true to him every day of his life, to pray for him, to worship your marriage, and to hold true these vows which you take today?"

"I do," Flora stated clearly with a saucy smile. She was rather looking forward to teasing Andrew about forgetting his one and only line in the wedding.

"The rings?" The priest motioned and Gwen passed Flora a ring of gold while Andrew took the delicate counterpart from his own pocket. "Now, repeat after me…with this ring, I thee wed."

"With this ring, I thee wed," they said in turn, each staring at their new rings.

The priest then closed his bible. "Then by the power invested in me by our Lord, I now pronounce you man and wife. You may kiss the bride."

Andrew cupped Flora's cheek and kissed her sweetly on the lips before the roaring audience. "I love you."

"And that's all the kiss I get?" she shot back, pulling him closer.

"Flora, wait until we're outside. Then I plan on doing a great many things to you," he whispered in a low voice that made her heart race in anticipation.

"Then we best hurry to make it back to the castle before the guests."

"Come, wife. I have a great many things I wish to do to you, and not much time in which to do them."

And together they ran from the chapel, their hands locked and souls bound, into the snow.

Acknowledgements

A special thank you to my editor, Rosa Sophia, who ensures my books aren't total hot messes, so I can be proud of the result.

And a hand to my lovely sorority sisters, who always have my back. SLAM!

About the Author

Kelsey McKnight is a university-educated historian from southern New Jersey. She has married her great loves of romance, history, and literature to create her first works that are set in Scotland. But she has recently begun to venture into the world of contemporary romance, drawing inspiration from true life. When she's not writing, Kelsey can be found reading, drinking too much coffee, blogging, spending time with her family, and working for two separate nonprofit organizations.

Facebook:
Facebook.com/Kissatmidnight

Twitter:
Twitter.com/KelseyMMcK

Website:
Kissatmidnight.wordpress.com

Instagram:
Instagram.com/akissatmidnight

Goodreads:
Goodreads.com/Kelsey_McKnight